THE GRAVE ROBBERS' CHRONICLES

VOL

The Grave Robbers' Chronicles:
Cavern of the Blood Zombies
By Xu Lei
Translated by Kathy Mok

Copyright©2011 ThingsAsian Press

Edited by Janet Brown and Michelle Wong
Illustrated by Neo Lok Sze Wong

For information regarding permissions, write to:
ThingsAsian Press
3230 Scott Street
San Francisco, California 94123 USA
www.thingsasianpress.com
Printed in China

ISBN-13: 978-1-934159-31-6
ISBN-10: 1-934159-31-X

TABLE OF CONTENTS

1. Fifty Years Ago…   5

2. Fifty Years Later…   13

3. Temple of Seeds   25

4. The Carcass Cave   36

5. The Shadow in the Water   48

6. The Unburied Dead   58

7. Hundreds of Heads   64

8. The Valley   72

9. The Ancient Tomb   82

10. The Shadow   91

11. Seven Coffins   100

12. The Door   107

13. 02200059.   110

14. Poker-face   118

15. Fart   124

16. A Small Green Hand   128

17. An Opening in the Cave   137

18. Tree of Death   142

19. The Female Corpse   149

20. The Key   154

21. The Green-Eyed Fox- Corpse   159

22. Disintegration of a Beautiful Corpse   168

23. Inner and Outer Coffins   172

24. Releasing the Zombie   182

25. The Jade Burial Armor   190

26. Secret of the Purple Jade Box   198

27. A Lie   207

28. Fire   217

29. The Purple-Enameled Gold Box   227

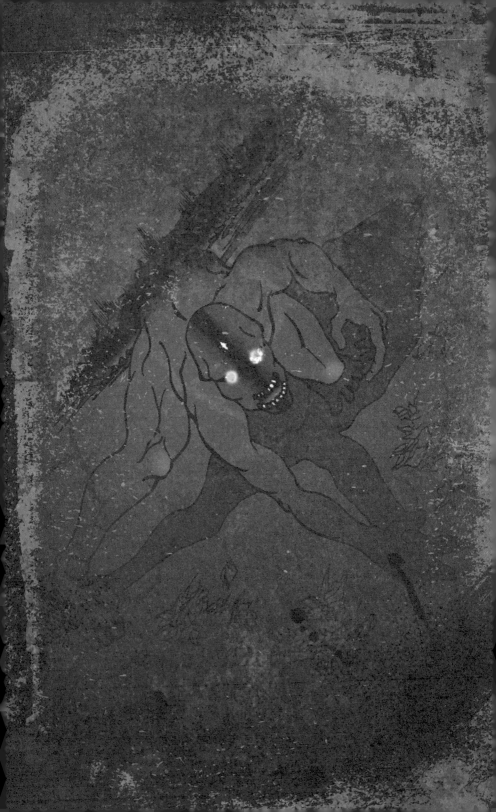

FIFTY YEARS AGO...

At the edge of an open grave squatted three men and a boy, all of them silent as they gaped at a shovel. This was a special sort of tool, known as a Luoyang shovel, used by men who loot burial sites. The long, tubular spade they had just pulled up from the grave was covered in dirt that oozed with a thick red liquid, as if the shovel had been dipped in blood.

The oldest man in the group stamped out his cigarette as he released an impatient cloud of smoke. "We're in big trouble. There's a zombie in that grave and if we aren't careful, we're all going to end up buried in there with it forever."

"What's wrong with you, Lao Yantou? You're always bitching about your old legs bothering you—are you too decrepit to go down into that grave?" said a one-eyed youth in his late teens. "We don't want to hear your bullshit—just give us a one-word answer, yes or no. If you won't go, my little brother and I are more than willing. Come on!"

Lao Yantou looked at the young man calmly and then turned to a big, bearded fellow standing nearby. "This son of yours has a bad attitude and a big mouth, grandson—you really need to teach him that in our trade loud words aren't enough to keep him from slipping and falling flat on his ass."

"You little bastard," the bearded man scowled at his son. "How dare you be so rude to your great-grandfather? He was robbing graves when you were still safe in your mother's belly."

"I was out of line," the one-eyed teenager apologized. "I spoke without thinking. But you know, if there's a zombie in that grave, it must be guarding treasure, and a lot of it. That's a good sign. We'd be stupid to leave without going down there. This is our chance to make ourselves rich and we can't ignore it."

"And now you dare to talk back to me?" The father raised his fist but Lao Yantou blocked his blow before it fell.

"Don't hit him—he's just the same as you were when you were young. If the upper beam of a house isn't straight, then the lower one is sure to be crooked too."

The teenager began to laugh as his father was reprimanded but Lou Yantou cuffed him on the side of his head. "What's so funny? Believe me, a zombie is no laughing matter. When we were working in Luoyang, one of your uncles dug up this same kind of bloody dirt and he's been a lunatic ever since, mumbling to himself all day, all night, with nobody understanding a word he says. Yes, we're going down into that grave and I'm going first." He nodded at his bearded grandson, "You follow me. One-eye, you go only as far as the first excavation level and your little brother had better stay out of the grave altogether. If all four of us are down there at one time, there isn't going to be enough room for us to get out fast if we need to. You, boy—One-eye here is going to hand you the rope after he ties it to this bucket—pull it up when you hear us yell."

"That's not fair," the boy grumbled. "Why do I have to stay out of the grave? I'm going to tell Mom you wouldn't let me go with you."

"Cheer up," laughed Lao Yantou. "Stop your fussing and Great-grandfather will find a nice little golden knife for you to play with, baby boy."

"I don't need you to find things for me. Let me go down into the grave and I'll find my own knife."

Grabbing his little brother by the ears, One-eye shook him as he yelled, "Why are you messing everything up for us and bothering Lau Yantou with your precious little tantrums, Mommy's boy? Even Mom wouldn't think you're so cute if she heard you whine like that. Shut up—if you say one more thing I'm going to kick your little sissy ass all the way back home to Mama where you belong."

"Cut it out!" Lao Yantou shouted. "We have work to do, stop squabbling—let's get at it," and he began to shovel dirt like a human whirlwind.

In half an hour, the grave opening had become a gaping abyss, and when the boy peered into the dark opening he could see nobody. One-eye emerged from time to time to get some fresh air but not a sound came from Lao Yantou or his bearded grandson.

It was dark and cold and lonely, waiting at the edge of the grave, and finally the boy called down into the depths, "Great-grandpa, have you found any treasures yet?" A few seconds passed before his brother's voice could be heard faintly, funneling up from the blackness, "No—we don't know. You, stay where you are—be sure to pull hard when we yell—pull that rope tight."

The boy heard a cough, and then Lao Yantou's whisper echoed in the dark, "Be quiet—listen! There's something's moving!" And then there was nothing but dead silence, leaving the boy terrified, unable to move or make a sound. Suddenly he heard an eerie rattling noise, as if a toad were calling from inside the grave, and then his older brother roared, "Pull, damn you, pull!"

The boy planted his feet as firmly as he could on the slippery ground, grabbed the rope that was tied to the bucket, and pulled with all of his strength, but then he felt resistance, as though something below had suddenly grabbed the other end. There was a giant tug and the rope was jerked back into the grave, with the boy almost going in with it.

Quickly he tied the end of the rope around his waist and leaned backward, almost touching the ground, using his entire weight to pull. This is how he always won at tug-of-war when he played with the other boys in his village and he knew he could exert enough force this way to hold his own even against a mule, if he had to. And sure enough, the boy was able to withstand whatever was trying to pull him into the pit, but the force on the other end was too powerful for him to pull the rope back up to the surface.

The sound of a gunshot came from within the grave and then his father's voice shouted, "Run, boy, run!"

1. FIFTY YEARS AGO...

The rope slackened and the bucket shot out of the pit. As the boy grabbed it, he thought he saw something clutching the rim but there was no time for him to look. Holding the bucket tightly in one hand, he ran as rapidly as he could, knowing something terrible was happening to his family in that open grave.

Only after a couple of miles did he stop to draw breath. As he released his grip on the bucket, he looked at it and screamed. Hooked on the rim was a severed hand, dripping blood. As he looked, the boy knew this was the hand of his one-eyed brother, who was now a cripple, if not a corpse.

I have to go back. I have to help my father and brother and Lao Yantou, he thought. He turned and there, sitting and staring at him, was a creature the color of blood.

This boy wasn't an ignoramus. He had gone on grave-robbing expeditions with his father many times before and in his short life had seen quite a few strange and unearthly things. He knew that anything could happen below the earth's surface and that the most important thing was never to panic, no matter how bizarre the circumstances might become. He knew that no murderous spirit could be stronger than any living person, and that anything, whether it be a black demon or a white devil, had to somehow comply with the law of physics. Once it was hit with a bullet and destroyed, the most terrifying ghost was nothing to be afraid of.

The boy always carried a pistol, an old box-gun his great-uncle had found in a warlord's tomb. He had never used it before but he knew what he had to do.

Stepping back, he pulled the pistol from his waistband and aimed at the creature before him. If this bloodred thing made a move toward him, he was ready to shoot.

The monster rose to its feet and as the boy looked at it, his scalp turned numb and his stomach churned violently. This creature was a man who had been skinned alive, as bloody and raw as if it had been squeezed out of its skin like a grape from its peel. How is it possible that this thing is still able to move? the boy wondered. Have I finally seen a blood zombie? Is this what they really look like?

As he stood frozen in shock, the boy saw the zombie hurl itself toward him, the smell of the blood dripping from its face and the sickly sour stench of its flesh wafting around its body like poison gas. The boy pulled the trigger of his pistol repeatedly and his volley of bullets struck the zombie's chest. Hit hard and spraying a fountain of blood, it reeled backward. The boy aimed at its head and squeezed the trigger again. This time the box-gun refused to fire; its ancient mechanism jammed.

With all of his strength, the boy hurled the useless gun at the zombie as hard as he could and raced away, not daring to look back at what might be following him. He sprinted toward a nearby tree, hoping that his pursuer would be unable to climb after him—and then he tripped, face flat against the tree trunk, his nose and mouth filled with blood.

How in the hell could I be so clumsy, he asked himself, beating the ground angrily with both fists. He heard the sound of thundering footsteps coming closer. He knew death was approaching, but, he thought, if I'm

1. FIFTY YEARS AGO...

going to die, I might as well die lying down. And then the zombie raced over the boy's body, leaving bloody footprints on his back. It kept running and faded away into the distance, still chasing the quarry that it had failed to see.

The zombie was surprisingly heavy, and with its first footstep the boy had felt as though its weight had squeezed all of the bile from his liver. His back began to itch with a tingling, burning sensation and everything before his eyes grew hazy. I've been poisoned, he thought, I'm going to die.

As his vision faded, all he could see was his brother's severed hand lying on the ground in front of him, with something clutched in its grasp. He blinked as hard as he could to see more clearly what was held in those dead fingers—it was a piece of glowing silk. My brother died to bring this up out of the grave, he thought, so it must be rare and valuable. I need to take care of it so even if I die, somebody will find what my brother found. Perhaps it will be important enough that neither of us will have died for no reason.

Painfully and slowly, the boy crawled to the hand, pried open the stiffened fingers, removed the piece of silk, and tucked it inside the sleeve of his own shirt. His ears began to buzz, his vision blurred as if a layer of wool had suddenly covered his eyes, and his hands and feet felt freezing cold. I just hope I don't pee and shit my pants, the boy told himself, people who are poisoned usually look disgusting when they die. I hope that pretty girl who always smiles at me in the village doesn't see how bad I look when they find my body and take it back home.

His thoughts raced wildly and began to make no sense, but through the buzzing that filled his ears, he could hear the same rattling sound he had heard coming from the grave before his brother had yelled at him to pull on the rope. What can this be? the boy wondered. The blood zombie didn't make a sound, even when I wounded it. Why do I hear this sound now? If it's not coming from the zombie that chased me, then what is making that noise?

His brain was no longer capable of giving orders to his body, but a reflex made him lift his head and focus his fading vision. There leaning toward him with a vacant stare was a gigantic, unearthly face. Its eyes had no pupils, and not the slightest spark of any sort of emotion came from their depths.

1. FIFTY YEARS AGO...

CHAPTER TWO
FIFTY YEARS LATER...

Half a century after all of this had taken place, as
I read these words at the Hangzhou Xiling Printing
Company, I was interrupted by someone coming through
the door. I closed my grandfather's journal, and looked
up to see an old man.

"Do you buy ancient books of ink inscriptions on silk
here?" he asked. It was a question I'm asked often since
I'm quite well-known in the antique book trade, and I
answered him with little interest, "Yes, but I don't pay
much for them." What I really meant was, if you don't
have anything good, get lost and let me go on with my
reading.

I was good enough at my line of work that I could
close my business for three years, then reopen it and
almost immediately make enough money to stay idle and
comfortable for another three years. I was used to doing
what I pleased during the day and had come to detest
customers who knew just a smattering about old books,
a loathing that increased over time. When I saw this sort
of person coming my way, I would put on an expression
of deepest boredom and shoo them away. But recently my
free time had been a little more than it should have been,

and the peak bookselling season would soon be over. There hadn't been much good stuff coming in, so I was a bit more eager than usual to do some business.

"In that case, I would like to ask if you have any silk books of ink inscriptions that date back to the Warring States Period? I'm especially interested in one found by some grave robbers fifty years ago that was later spirited out of the country by an American," the man asked, peering at the books displayed on my counter.

"If it were taken away by an American, then how could I have it?" I replied, annoyed at what seemed a pointless request. "If you're looking for volumes like that, go to the antique market and don't bother me. How could you be so stupid as to think you could find this particular book? Who would ever be able to put their hands on it?"

He lowered his voice. "I heard you had the money and the connections. You were recommended to me by Lao Yang."

Suddenly I snapped to attention, wildly alert. Didn't Lao Yang go to prison just a year ago? Why was he blabbing about me from his cell? My heart raced and cold sweat rolled down my back. "Which…what Lao Yang? I don't know who you're talking about."

"I know, I know." He smiled and took a watch out of his shirt pocket. "Take a look. Lao Yang said you'd understand once you saw this."

Lao Yang had been given that watch by his first love when he was up in the Northeast, and he treated her gift as if it were as valuable as his own life. Many times when he was drunk, he would take the watch out, look at it, and call out "Azalea! My beautiful girl!" I once asked him what on earth he was yelling about, and he was silent for a long time, then out of the blue began to sob and told me he couldn't remember. If Lao Yang had given his watch to this old man, that was a clear indication that he thought this stranger was someone worthy of my attention.

Nonetheless, as I looked at the man in front of me, I thought he was nothing more than a hideous old pain in the ass. But since he had approached me with Lao Yang's most treasured possession, I thought it best to make him think that I spoke frankly and openly. Raising both of my hands clasped into one fist as a gesture of respect and mutual trust, I asked, "So you are a friend of Lao Yang's. Why do you want to see me?"

The old man grinned widely, exposing a large gold tooth. "I have a friend from Shanxi who brought back something from there. I'd like for you to take a look at it and tell me if it's real."

"I can tell from your accent you're from up north. You're a big wheel from Beijing who's come south to ask advice from me—I am so flattered. But why? There are many expert appraisers in Beijing. I'm afraid the drinker's heart is not in the cup!"

He laughed, "Ha! When people say that Southerners are intuitive, they are absolutely right. I see that you're a young man but you are already very perceptive and you speak the truth. Indeed, I did not hope to see you on this visit. I came to see the elderly gentleman in your household."

My expression changed at once. "Looking for my grandfather? What do you want?"

"Do you know if there were any other books made at the same time as the silk book of the Warring States Period that your grandfather stole from that grave fifty years ago? My friend wants to know if the volume we have is from that historical period."

Before he finished speaking, I was already shouting at my salesclerk who dozed at the other end of the counter, "Wang Meng, show this visitor out!"

The old man looked confused. "Why do you shoo me away when I'm still talking?"

"What you said about my grandfather is true, but you have come too late. He died last year. If you want to find him, go away and kill yourself!"

As I yelled, I thought to myself, what happened a half-century ago was so dreadful that it shocked even government officials. Why would I ever let this old fart rummage through the past to stir up that old story again? If all that came back into the public eye, how could anyone ever think well of my family again?

"Young grandson, how quickly your speech turns from sweet to sour!" The old man showed his gold tooth again in an evil grin. "It matters little that the old gentleman has passed on. I'm not asking too much of you. Why don't you just take a look at what I brought, if only so Lao Yang won't lose face, eh?"

I looked at him as he forced himself to put on an insincere smile and realized he'd probably never go away unless I took a peek at whatever he had. I supposed I ought to do this just to save Lao Yang's face and to keep him from berating me the next time I saw him.

I nodded. "I'll take a look but I can't guarantee the

authenticity of your piece."

I knew there was a collection of more than twenty silk volumes written in ink from the Warring States Period, and that each volume was different from the rest. The chapter that my grandfather had taken from a grave was only a fragment of just one volume, but still it was extremely important. I had a few of these volumes packed away in the bottom of boxes and they were my dearest treasures, which I wouldn't trade for all the money on the face of the earth.

The old man with the gold tooth took a piece of white cloth out of his breast pocket. As soon as I saw it I felt even more annoyed—hell, it had to be fake.

"Oh, this precious thing really shouldn't have been traveling around in hiding like that. It'll fall into shreds if it's just given a little shake," he said, lowering his voice to seem mysterious and secretive. "If it weren't for my connections, this piece would have gone overseas long ago. I suppose my keeping it here in our country is at the very least a service to the Chinese people."

I laughed in his face. "Looks like you're a grave robber yourself! I bet you don't dare to sell it because it's a national treasure. Who would want to lose his head in a public execution?"

I seemed to have struck upon the truth because the old man's face turned green. But because he needed a favor from me, he ignored my rudeness.

"That is not precisely true," he said mildly. "Every trade has its own honorable standards. Everyone remembers that when your grandfather was a grave robber, his awe-inspiring reputation for ethical behavior was known far and wide."

Now my own complexion lost its normal color and I spoke through clenched teeth. "If you mention my grandfather again, you can get the hell out and take your treasure with you."

"Okay, okay. I'll stop. Just take a quick look, so I can be on my way."

When I unfolded the piece of white cloth, I knew immediately that this was a well-preserved volume of the silk books from the Warring States Period, but it was certainly not the one my grandfather had stolen in Changsha. It looked like a counterfeit made a few dynasties after the original had been created. That was to say, this was an ancient forgery, and such an object would only embarrass anyone who possessed it.

I smiled. "This looks like a counterfeit of the Han dynasty. How can I say this…it's fake, but at the same time it's not. It's real, but at the same time it also isn't. How the hell can anybody tell if it's a copy of an original volume or just a careful fabrication of something that never existed? I don't know what to say."

"So is it like the one your grandfather stole?"

"To be honest with you, my grandfather himself didn't even take a good look at the one he stole before the American swindled him out of it. I really can't answer your question." It was hard enough to sway you from your initial confidence in what you brought me, I thought, and now I even have to pretend that I give a damn about you or what you have carried in here. But the old man with the gold tooth seemed to have no doubts about my sincerity as he sighed, "What bad luck for me. If I can't find an American who's stupid enough to buy this, then there really is no hope of my making any money from it."

"How come you're so concerned about this particular volume?" I asked.

"I won't hide the truth from you, young fellow. I'm no grave robber. Look at my bony old body—it's neither fast nor agile. But my friend is really an expert and I have no idea what kind of game he's playing. In any case, every man has his own reasons for what he does." He smiled and shook his head. "I better quit asking questions and take off," and he began to walk away without looking back.

I looked down, and realized I still had his piece of silk in my hands. Suddenly I could see something imprinted on the sheet, a foxlike face of a man. His two eyes had no pupils and looked three-dimensional, as if they were convex forms protruding from the cloth. I gasped and took a deep breath. I had never seen anything like this before, and I was sure it must be a valuable treasure. Once Lao Yang got out of prison, we could make a few counterfeits from this piece, just enough to keep me amused—and solvent. I hurried outside, looked around, and saw the old man with the gold tooth scurrying back in my direction.

He must be coming back to retrieve his piece of silk, I thought, so I quickly went back inside, grabbed my digital camera, snapped a few photos of the cloth, and headed out the door. My face almost hit the tip of the old man's nose. "You forgot something," I said.

My grandfather was a "dirt prowler," as it was commonly termed, a grave robber. The reason he went into this trade was not surprising. It was what we would call today a family business. The year my great-grandfather's great-grandfather turned thirteen, a severe drought plagued Changsha in central China and famine naturally followed. Even people with money were starving to death.

There was nothing in the streets or in any corner of Changsha that could be used to make a living except for the ancient tombs that could be found there. And as the saying goes, those living on a mountain will survive by using what they can find on the mountain; those who have nothing but graves nearby will rob the graves to stay alive. Only heaven knows how many people died from starvation in Changsha during those years, except for those from my grandfather's village, who were all well-fed and well-dressed. And that was only possible because they used what they dug from the graves to barter with foreigners for food.

After some time had passed, just as in other trades, grave robbing also began to acquire its own rules and techniques. By the time my grandfather's generation took up the job, grave robbers were divided into two groups, the northern and the southern factions. My grandfather belonged to the southern faction, who were experts at excavating soil by using the Luoyang shovel. The most talented of them all could ascertain the depth and the age of the soil above a tomb simply through their sense of smell.

The northern faction would never use the Luoyang shovel, but were still very good at figuring out the exact location and the structure of the tombs, a difficult skill few people could attain.

There was something strange about the northern faction. According to my grandfather, too many of them were sly and deceitful. As if robbing a grave wasn't enough to do, they had to create different rituals to observe such as kowtowing to the dead, which led to an overwhelming bureaucracy overseeing the trade. In contrast, the southern faction had few regulations and was unconcerned about offending the dead.

The northern faction claimed the southerners were pretentious and conceited, denounced them as a disgrace to their culture, and said that every grave robbed by a southerner was left in a state of complete ruin. They spread rumors that southern grave robbers even dragged out the dead bodies and put the corpses up for sale.

The southern faction called the northerners hypocrites and no more than thieves who posed as honorable men. The conflict escalated to the boiling point, so much so that "a battle for corpses" took place and in the end, the two factions were divided by terminology as much as they were by the Yangtze River. The northern faction called the trade "tomb raiding," while the southern faction called it "digging up the soil."

The Luoyang shovel wasn't invented until after the two factions had completely severed all connections, so the northern grave robbers refused to lower themselves by touching a shovel that had been invented by southerners.

When he was young, my grandfather did not know how to read; he only knew how to rob graves. Later, he took some literacy classes, even though for him learning a new word was as bad as being tortured. But thanks to his education, he was able to record his adventures.

He was the young boy who wounded the blood zombie fifty years ago. He wrote about this and all else that had happened in his journal, in his own words and in his own hand. My grandmother was an intellectual, the daughter of an illustrious and well-respected family. She was deeply attracted to my grandfather's stories and fell in love with him. My grandfather married her and settled down in Hangzhou, and his journal became a family treasure.

As for how he had survived the Changsha ordeal, or what became of his older brother, their father, or Lao Yantou, my grandfather refused to tell me. He would weep when I asked about this and say, "That is not a story for children." No matter how sweetly I asked, or how charmingly I begged for details, he would not utter even half a word about it. As I grew up, my childhood curiosity faded, but as far as I can remember, I never saw a great-uncle who had only one eye and one hand.

On the day that I met the old man with the gold tooth, I closed the shop early and sent my salesclerk home. Before I locked up for the night, a text message came in on my cell phone: "9 o'clock, Huangsha Chicken-Eye."

It was from my father's third brother, Uncle Three, in a secret code that meant a new shipment had arrived. Another message closely followed: "Spine of a dragon. Come quickly."

2. FIFTY YEARS LATER...

My eyes sparkled. My Uncle Three had an unusually keen intuition. "Spine of a dragon" meant something exceptional had come his way. Anything he deemed exceptional I had to see for myself.

Quickly I drove to my uncle's place. On one hand, I wanted to have a look at what this good stuff was. On the other hand, I wanted to show him the photos I had just taken and see if he could tell me anything about the figure on the cloth. I hoped he could since he was the only person I knew who had any direct contact with the past generation of grave robbers.

As I drew near the stairway of his building, I heard him shouting from above, "You goddamn kid. Told you to hurry up, and then you take ages. What use is there for you to show up now?"

"Shit," I yelled back, "are you serious? You had good stuff and you didn't even wait for me to take a look at it? Why did you have to sell it so fast?"

As I said this, a young man walked out my uncle's front door, carrying a long object on his back that was wrapped tightly in a piece of cloth. At first glance I could tell it was part of an ancient weapon. Obviously it was very valuable, and no matter what the man had paid my uncle, it could probably be resold for ten times what he given Uncle Three for it.

I pointed to the young man, and Uncle nodded and shrugged. I felt a stab of despair, wondering how much our capital would dwindle with these kinds of business deals and if my shop might go bankrupt this year as a result.

I walked upstairs, made myself a cup of coffee, and

told my uncle about the old man with the gold tooth who had come to pry into our family history. I was certain Uncle Three, famous for his quick temper, would share my anger toward the man who had annoyed me so much. Instead my uncle assumed an unfamiliar, benign personality and calmly printed out the photos on my digital camera. As he put them under the light for a closer look, I was able to see the change of expression that washed over his face.

"What's going on?" I asked. "What's the matter?"

Frowning, he muttered, "It can't be...this looks like a map of the ancient tombs!"

CHAPTER THREE

THE TEMPLE OF SEEDS

I looked at the pictures I'd taken and then back at my uncle's face. It didn't look like he was kidding around. Was it possible that Uncle Three had reached the point where he could see a map drawn in a portion of text? It was hard to see any proof of extrasensory perception in this crazy guy who cared for nothing but eating, drinking, gambling, and visiting prostitutes.

Yet I could see he was excited by what he saw in my photos—he shuddered as he said to himself, "How did these people get a hold on such a magnificent piece while I have never been so lucky? This is truly good fortune. It looks like they still haven't figured out what they have. We can still catch up and go far beyond them before they even begin to dig up the ground."

I was completely confused, "Uncle, perhaps I'm a bit of an imbecile—but can you really see a map in the midst of such tiny words?"

"You don't have a clue about what I see here. This is called script mapping—that means the details of the location and the geography of the place are written down and described in words. Other common people probably wouldn't be able to read this. But thank heaven for me, your uncle, who still has something called experience. On the entire face of the earth, I'm positive that no more than ten individuals—apart from me—could read this."

My Uncle Three didn't know a lot but from an early age, he had studied many unusual, eccentric, and unorthodox ancient texts and code words. To summarize, whatever was exotic he learned to analyze. The Five Illustrations of the Wooden Text from Xixia; the earliest Nuzhen Ya characters—it was nothing for him to explain these things clearly and talk about them in knowledgeable detail. That he knew what this arcane script painting was surprised me not one bit.

But he was also the type of guy who liked to refuse to explain what he knew, bragging on and on about his cleverness. If I wanted to find out what he had discovered, I needed to play the part of a humble halfwit. Looking as naïve as possible, I asked, "Oh, so does it say to turn left and then turn right, then at the tree ahead turn right again, and once you see a well then make your way down into it? Is it that sort of thing?"

Uncle sighed. "Who can teach an idiot? Your comprehension skills are so poor. As far as I can see, our family went right downhill after you came into it."

"What are you saying? My father didn't teach me any of this stuff and it certainly isn't anything I was born knowing."

"Listen carefully," he gloated, "this type of script mapping is in fact a kind of secret code. It has a strict format, and if you can draw what the text describes according to that format, you then will have a whole and complete map. So don't badmouth this piece of cloth. Who knows what sort of detailed information it contains—it might even tell the exact number of bricks to be found in a specific area."

I was intrigued. Never in my life had anyone in my family ever let me accompany them on a grave robbing expedition. But this time Uncle Three had to take me with him so I could enlarge my body of experience, grab a few treasures, and get out of my current economic crisis. As I contemplated this scenario, I asked, "Can you tell from the writing whose grave it refers to? Maybe it's some historical figure who had power and influence."

Uncle smiled boastfully. "I can't completely understand it all right now. But it looks like this grave belonged to one of the nobles from the State of Lu during the Warring States Period. Just from seeing that the location of his grave was recorded on silk with such a complex type of script mapping, I can say that this person's status was extremely high. What's more, that his burial ground was so heavily concealed implies that there it holds plenty of riches. It is certainly worth a visit."

I was amazed to see the glow in his eyes. On an ordinary day, this old guy was too lazy to step out the door of his own house. Could he possibly want to search for this grave himself? If so, I thought, that would be another strange piece of family lore that would echo through the ages. "Uncle," I asked, "do you really intend to go and dig up this plot of soil?"

Patting me on the shoulder, he looked at me condescendingly and said, "It's all right. You just don't know. Let me tell you: the graves of the five dynasties of Tang, Song, Yuan, Ming, and Qing certainly have treasures, but those can only be described as treasures with superb craftsmanship that excel anything found in nature. The Warring States Period was an era containing royal tombs from long-distant centuries. You would never be able to imagine what was put in those graves. The objects in the tombs of this period are things that glorified the powerful rulers of that time and represent the supreme glories of an unknown age. They are things that no longer exist in the living world! How could I not want to have a look for myself?"

"Are you so sure? Perhaps there is nothing inside this grave."

"That's impossible. Didn't you see this pattern?" He pointed to the bizarre foxlike face. "This is from the earliest times of the State of Lu, the mask that a person wore when they were ceremoniously sacrificed in a funeral rite. The person buried in this grave must have enjoyed an exceptional status—maybe even more distinguished than the emperor's at that time."

I blurted out, "Oh, bullshit."

Uncle gave me a reproving look and moved to put away the photos. Pressing my hands down on the pictures before he could pick them up, I smiled at him. "Uncle, don't rush to put these away. Remember I was the one who took these photos in the first place. You must take me with you to see everything you've just described to me—it's only fair."

"Impossible!" he shouted. "Digging up this grave is not as simple as you might think. You'll find no air-conditioning in a tomb, just layer after layer of elaborate traps which could end the whole adventure in a heartbeat.

You are your father's only child. If anything should happen to you, your old dad would without a doubt skin me alive."

"Then screw it! Pretend that I never came!" I quickly grabbed the photos, turned around and walked away. I knew my Uncle Three well. Once he came across something that interested him, whether it was an antique or a woman, he would abandon every principle he had. I aimed with precision at this personality flaw and sure enough, I had gone only a few steps when he surrendered.

Running up to me, he pulled at the photos in my hand. "Well, all right, fine, okay. You've got me. But let's make one thing clear right now. When we're down in the grave, you stay above ground. Do you understand?"

Soaring with excitement, I thought, When the time comes, if I insist on going with you, what will you be able to do to stop me? But I nodded enthusiastically. "You have my word! When we're off on this adventure, I will obey you to the end. I will do whatever you say!"

Uncle had no choice. He sighed and said, "We can't do this with just the two of us. I'll arrange for a few experienced men to come over tomorrow and I'll spend the next few days deciphering this script mapping. Your job is to go and buy some things for me." He rapidly wrote a list, handed it to me, and said, "Be sure not to buy anything of poor quality and don't forget to buy any item on this list. If we don't have everything we need for our trip we could be sunk before we even reach the gravesite."

The things that Uncle Three wanted weren't easy to find. It seemed as though he was deliberately trying to make this a difficult task for me, because none of the things on his list were commonly stocked in most stores. He wanted waterproof miner's lamps that could be taken apart for easy transport, soil-testing shovels, Swiss Army knives, folding shovels, short-handled hammers, bandages, nylon ropes, and much more. After buying only half of the supplies on his list, I had already spent a small fortune that came out of my own pocket. Mourning my shrinking bank account, I cursed my uncle for using my money when he had plenty of his own—the miserly old bastard.

Three days later, five of us—Uncle Three; Panzi and Big Kui, who were two of his old grave-robbing partners; the young man whom I had seen leaving my uncle's house with the purchased antique the night I came over with the photos; and I—arrived at the location shown on the script mapping, about a hundred kilometers west of the Temple of Seeds in Shandong.

How can I describe this place? The best I can say about it is there was nothing there. To reach it, first we traveled in a long-distance motor coach, then in a much less comfortable long-distance bus, then on long-distance motorcycles, and then in wagons pulled by cattle.

When we got off the cattle carts, we could see nothing in any direction. A dog ran toward us and Uncle Three patted the shoulder of the old man whom he had hired to be our guide. "Sir, are we going to ride on this dog next? I'm afraid carrying all of us will be quite a burden for him."

"Of course not," the old man laughed. "This dog is a messenger. For the final leg of your journey, there's no land transport—you have to go by boat, and the dog will bring the boat to you."

3. THE TEMPLE OF SEEDS

"So he can swim, can he?"

"He swims pretty fine, pretty fine…" The old man looked at the dog. "Donkey Egg, show these gentlemen what you can do!"

The dog jumped into the river and swam around in a circle. When he came out of the water, he shook his fur dry and lay close by, panting.

"It's still too early right now. The boatman definitely hasn't started work yet. We'll take a break and smoke a cigarette first."

I looked at my watch. "It's two in the afternoon and the boatman hasn't started working? What kind of schedule does he stick to?"

"He's the only boatman around in these parts and he's one hell of a shrewd bastard. He starts working whenever he decides to get up and there are some days he doesn't work at all. It irritates the shit out of the eager explorers who come to visit the cave," the old man said with a smile. "There's no other way to get there. The River God will allow only him to take you to the cave that you want to find. Anyone else who enters that place is certain never to return—anyone else but him. If you guys want to go by mule, then we can travel past the hills and go to the cave that way but that will take at least another day. And you guys have so much stuff—even if we use all the mules in our entire village, there wouldn't be enough of them to carry all that you have."

"I see." The minute Uncle heard the word "cave," his spirits instantly ran high and he took out the map he had decoded. He had been handling this like his most prized possession, and would not let me take even one peek.

When we saw him bring it to light, we crowded in to check it out, all but the young fellow who had bought the antique from my uncle. He sat off by the side and kept quiet.

To tell the truth, I didn't care for this guy at all. Panzi and Big Kui, the two men who used to work with my uncle, were friendly, steady, reliable fellows. But this young guy didn't so much as fart once on the entire journey—he was like a deaf-mute. All he did was look straight up at the sky, as if he were worried that it was going to fall down on him. When we first began our trip I talked to him a bit but after a while I didn't bother to pay any attention to him at all. I honestly couldn't understand why my uncle brought this obnoxious poker-faced jerk along with us.

"There is a cave, a river cave, right at the back of this mountain," Uncle Three said. "So what's the deal, old man? Does this cave eat people alive?"

The old man smiled. "It's all talk passed down from the older generation. I can't remember all the exact details. People in the village used to say there was a snake monster in there. And that those who went in the cave never came out. Then one day, the boatman's great-grandfather paddled a small boat out from inside the cave. He told us he was a traveling salesman from out of town. But who ever saw a traveling salesman carrying a boat on his shoulders while he ran around doing business? Everyone said he was the snake monster transformed into a human. When he heard that, he laughed it off and said he bought the boat from people in the next village and if we didn't believe him, just go and ask. So people went and asked, and the answer was just as he claimed. So everybody believed him, and thought the monster in the cave was gone. Then a few adventurous teenagers went into the cave, and never came out.

From that day on, only the family of the traveling salesman was able to go in and come out without being harmed. Don't you think that's strange? Later on, through the years, his family kept running this business, all the way up to now."

"Can the dog take messages in there and return unscathed?" I was intrigued by this story.

"This is their family dog. But other people's dogs or livestock that go into the cave never come out."

"And the government doesn't investigate something so baffling and bizarre?"

"How many people believe us when we talk about it?" The old man tapped the spent ashes from his pipe onto the ground.

Uncle Three frowned and clapped his hands. "Donkey Egg, come over here."

The dog wagged his tail and came running over obediently. Uncle picked him up and sniffed him, and his expression changed. "That can't be…is it possible this is in the cave?"

I also picked the animal up and sniffed. I choked and coughed at the overwhelmingly foul smell. This dog's master was quite a slacker. Heaven knew how long it had been since the dog had a bath.

Panzi burst into laughter. "If you want to follow in your uncle's footsteps, you still have a long way to go!"

"This goddamn dog stinks!" I smiled while I struggled not to vomit.

"This dog grew up eating dead human meat," Uncle Three said. "That's a cave filled with people's carcasses. That boatman the old man is talking about, I'm afraid when he was a child, he too was fed…"

"Oh no—that can't be!" I was so scared that my hair stood on end. Even young Poker-face's expression changed a bit when he heard this.

Big Kui, Uncle Three's other buddy, was a whale of a man whose head was almost as big as those of the cattle that pulled the cart, but inside he was a timid, fearful wimp. He asked so softly that it was almost a whimper, "What do you mean about this cave? Will we be in danger when we go in there?"

"I don't know. But a few years ago in Taiyuan, Shanxi, I found a cave like that where bodies were piled up during the Japanese massacre. Wherever you find a carcass cave, it's a place where there has probably been a massacre—this I am certain of. You know," he added thoughtfully, "I heard of a place in Shanxi where people fed dead human flesh to kids when they were little so the stink of corpses would accumulate in their bodies. When the kids grew up, their bodies smelled just like a dead man's and not even ghosts couldn't tell the difference between them and a corpse. Sir, was your traveling salesman who became a boatman from Shanxi?"

The old man's expression flickered and he shook his head. "I have no idea! That was this boatman's great-grandfather and that was long before my time." He looked up into the sky, and said to the dog, "Donkey Egg, go and get the boat from your house!" The dog plunged into the water and swam toward the back of the mountain.

Meanwhile, I saw Uncle Three look quickly at Panzi, who stealthily took a backpack out of the pile of luggage and put it on his back while Poker-face did the same. Panzi walked past me, whispering, "We may not be able to trust this old man— watch out."

3. THE TEMPLE OF SEEDS

CHAPTER FOUR
THE CARCASS CAVE

My Uncle Three had worked with Panzi and Big
Kui for years in a trade more dangerous than most.
The three of them were all experienced grave robbers
who knew what they were doing and I trusted them
completely. So when Panzi told me to watch out, I knew
where things stood.

Big Kui gave me a quick look that told me to keep
quiet and stay out of any trouble that might crop up. I
smiled in response while thinking, why would I need to
get involved anyway? Big Kui was capable of knocking
down a cow with one punch without even trying, and
Panzi was a war veteran with scars all over his body. My
Uncle Three, from the time he was young, was famous
for being devil-may-care when he got into fistfights—
plus that quiet poker-faced bastard didn't look one
bit like a merciful type. And then there was me, the
intellectual—since time began, eggheads like me were
notorious for being useless in a brawl.

Uncle Three came beside me and jammed an army
knife into my hand. It was heavy and felt unnatural
and awkward. I had no idea of how to use it if I had to
defend myself.

At that moment Donkey Egg swam back and leaped to shore with a splash. The old man hit his pipe against his trousers and said, "Let's go! The boat's here."

Two boats emerged from the back of the mountain, one after the other. A middle-aged man stood on the first vessel, shouting as he poled it toward us. It was a good-sized boat that looked like it had more than enough space for our equipment. The old man patted the cow's neck. "Gentlemen, there is no need to unload and move your gear. I'll pull the cow and the cart onto the second boat, and we'll all ride on the first one. That will be easier for everybody."

Panzi smiled. "Some of our stuff isn't waterproof and I think it would be better to carry those things with us. If the cow jumped into the water, wouldn't we be screwed?"

The old man smiled and nodded. "You have a point. But our cow here is not a buffalo. It would never jump into the water. If it did jump, I myself would personally help you rescue your things until every single item was retrieved."

Quickly and skillfully, the middle-aged boatman guided both boats ashore. The old man pulled the cow toward the boats while we each shouldered our own bags and followed behind him.

While the cow and cart were being loaded onto the second boat, I checked out the boatman. His complexion was dark and swarthy and he had a rough appearance; somehow I felt he was up to no good. I remembered what Uncle Three said about people who ate the flesh from dead bodies, and all of a sudden the man looked ghastly and horrifying.

"When we're at the cave, everyone, be sure to whisper, so as not to upset the River God—and be careful—do not speak ill of him," the boatman warned us.

"How long does it take to reach the cave?" Uncle Three asked.

"If we're very lucky, we'll get there in five minutes. The river's current is very swift and dangerous, especially inside the cave."

"So there are spots where it's not so strong?"

"Yes. Sometimes the water goes upstream. When you saw me rowing down, it was going downstream. Now we'll have to go against the current, which could take us much longer, perhaps around fifteen minutes. There are also a few dangerous turns to negotiate along the way."

"Is it light inside the cavern?"

The man laughed. "No sun reaches into that place—how could there be any light? You could say it's completely pitch-black." Then he pointed to his ears. "I have been a boatman for decades. These punt-poles and my ears are good enough to get me by."

"In that case, can I use a flashlight?" Panzi raised the miner's lamp in his hand. "It won't obstruct your view, will it?"

"Not at all," the man said. "But be sure not to shine it into the water. You'll be scared to death!"

"Why?" Uncle Three smiled. "Is there a water monster of some sort?"

"Not even a water monster could compare to what's there. I don't even want to talk about it. If you guys are daredevils, take a look—but remember, just one glance is enough. If you're lucky, all you'll see is a pool of black water. If you're not, what's there will scare the hell out of you."

As he spoke, we could see the cave at a distance, hidden at the base of the cliffs. When we were on the shore, we couldn't see a thing, and imagined it would be a gigantic cavern. But as we got closer, we were surprised to see that it was actually tiny, with an entrance so small that it was only about four inches wider than the boat we were on. But the most alarming thing about this portal was its height. Men couldn't go through it even if they were sitting down. If we crouched with bent backs, we would only manage to enter with enormous effort. If anyone inside meant us any harm, it would be impossible for us to move our arms and legs to defend ourselves in such a small, compressed space.

"Holy shit," Panzi cried, "isn't this cave a little bit cramped?"

"It's fairly large. There is a passage inside that's even narrower than this," the old man said from the back of the boat.

Uncle Three shot Panzi a look, and Panzi smiled. "Ah. If there was someone in the cave trying to rob us, I guess he wouldn't be able to escape easily with so little room, eh?"

At this point, I saw the middle-aged boatman move his hand as though in some sort of signal, and the old man's expression changed. I thought to myself, there certainly is something going on here. Then we heard a roar, and the boat shot into the cave.

Panzi turned on his miner's lamp. At first we could

still see light from the outside but soon our lamp became the only source of illumination.

"Master Three, this cave isn't so simple, huh?" Big Kui said. "This is a water robbers' cavern!"

"A water robbers' cavern…Unlike modern caves which are dug with a rectangular entrance to the underground world, this entrance is circular which tells us this is an ancient cave. When we go in here, we may well enter another kind of world."

"Oh. This gentleman apparently is quite experienced. He's right," said the boatman, who leaned forward and knelt with one knee resting on the bow. He was paddling with just one hand as if he were drawing a dot here and a stroke there. But the strange thing was that his pole did not touch the water at all, nor was he out of breath as he should have been after paddling upstream with a group of men on board his boat.

"I've heard that this entire mountain was a tomb," he said. "There are many of these water caves nearby, all different sizes, but this one is the largest and the deepest. I think in time past, the water was not this high; perhaps this might even have been a dry cave."

"Oh. Apparently you're also an expert." Uncle Three politely handed the boatman a cigarette, who accepted it as he shook his head and said, "Expert? Give me a break. I've only heard this from the people who came here before me. I heard more and more stories, and eventually learned how to say a few things here and there. My knowledge is slight. Please don't mock me by calling me an expert."

Panzi and Big Kui both had their hands on their

knives as my uncle and the boatman continued their banter. Although the atmosphere seemed pleasant and harmonious, everyone in our group was on edge. There were five of us and only two of them so if anything were to happen, I reckoned we probably would not be the losers. On the other hand, if these two dared to attack us, that would certainly mean they had come well-prepared, ready to overpower us.

As I continued with my thoughts, the poker-faced young fellow waved his hand. "Hush! Listen, someone is talking!"

We all held our breath, and we could hear a voice coming from deep within the cave. We strained to make out what was being said but could only occasionally decipher a word or two. I turned to ask the boatman whether he often heard these sounds when he was here but to my surprise, I found that he had disappeared. I turned to the other side of the boat, and shit—the old man had vanished as well.

"Panzi, where did they go?" Uncle Three cried.

"Don't know. Didn't hear any diving sounds," Panzi was also astonished. "The minute we heard that voice, I stopped paying attention to those guys."

"Oh my god, we don't smell like corpses. What's going to happen to us? Panzi, you fought in Vietnam back in the day. Did you ever eat the liver of your enemies?" my uncle demanded.

"You've got to be kidding, Master Three, I was in the kitchen washing dishes every day." Panzi pointed to Big Kui. "Fatty, didn't you say your family used to sell buns stuffed with human meat long ago? You're such a greedy bastard—you must have eaten a lot of those when you were a kid."

"Bullshit! I made that up. Besides, we made those human meat buns to make money from other people. Have you ever seen a salesman so desperate that he'd eat his own wares?"

I quickly made a time-out signal. "The three of you put together add up to being older than a century and a half. Stop being such jerks and show us young guys a good example, will you?"

Just as I finished speaking, the boat quivered and Panzi grabbed his lamp. He flashed it toward the water and when the light hit the current, we saw a monstrous shadow swimming past us.

Big Kui's face turned white as he pointed at the water. His jaw dropped and he was unable to utter a word. He looked as though he was ready to pass out, and Uncle Three gave him a hard slap on the face. "You son of a bitch!" he shouted. "It's only a trick of the light. The two young guys didn't even blink but you who have worked for me all these years—you freak out for no reason. Eat shit, you fucking idiot."

"Master Three, you saw that thing—it's a goddamn monster. All five of us wouldn't make a meal for that humongous creature."

It was plain to see that Big Kui's heart was still pounding with fear as he stared at the water. He had been sitting near the side of the boat, but now his butt had moved to the center, as if he was afraid something might suddenly surge out of the river and drag him down, away from us all.

4. THE CARCASS CAVE

"Piss on you!" Uncle Three stared at him viciously. "We are men who take and keep whatever we want from whomever we want. You know me—I'm Old Master Three of the Wu family, who have robbed graves for generations. I've come across every kind of monster you can think of in my life and I'm still drawing breath. Stop talking like a frightened child and remember who you are and who you work for."

We were all speechless, not because of fear, but from realizing that there was such a behemoth under the surface of the water in such a narrow and cramped space. For a few minutes none of us could think clearly or say a word until Panzi broke the silence. "Master Three, this cave is weird and it creeps me out so much I don't know my ass from my elbow right this minute. Let's get out of here for a quick break and talk things over. How does that sound?"

Big Kui couldn't agree fast enough. I was shaken too and wanted to get out of this cave as soon as possible. But on the other hand, Uncle Three was my blood relative and my father's brother. No matter what, I needed to let him speak up before I said what was on my mind.

To my surprise, Uncle Three looked over at Poker-face as if he wanted that guy's opinion. From all I had ever seen of my uncle, he wouldn't even ask advice from any god in heaven—or pay attention if they gave it to him. But now he seemed to be deferring to this young twerp. I couldn't help but wonder what was up and turned to see what Poker-face might have to say, but it was plain that he wasn't listening at all. He was staring straight into the water, as if he were focusing all of his attention on finding whatever it was that we had just seen.

I wanted to ask Uncle Three where the hell this man came from but this didn't seem like the right time, so I asked Panzi very quietly. He shook his head and said he wasn't sure. All he knew was that he was sharp and resourceful. He gestured to the guy's right hand with his chin and said, "You see his hand? Imagine how many years it would take to develop that."

I really had not noticed Poker-face's hand but when I looked, I discovered it was indeed very unusual. His middle and index fingers were exceptionally long, which I knew came from the art of exploring soil by using only those two fingers.

This was a rare skill that I had read about in my grandfather's journal. It was invented in ancient times by master grave robbers who had fingers as steady and as unwavering as the most solid mountain. With their strong and dexterous fingers these masters could easily disable all the little traps that had been placed in the tombs. Learning this unique skill involved years of a long and miserable martyrdom of practice that began in early childhood.

As I looked at Poker-face, wondering just what he was capable of doing with those fingers, he raised his right arm and thrust it into the water at lightning speed. When he drew his hand back to the water's surface, there was a bug held tightly between his two freakishly long fingers. He threw it on the deck, saying, "This was what we saw just now."

I lowered my head to take a closer look, and sighed in

relief. "Isn't this a water beetle? So the monster's shadow we saw a moment ago was just a mass of these water beetles swimming below us?"

"That's right," he replied as he wiped his hands on his clothes.

Although we weren't sure this was true, it made us all feel better and Big Kui stepped on the bug, squashing it flat.

But as I considered this, it didn't seem plausible. How could there be so many water beetles moving at the same time? What's more, the head of that water monster was way too big to be only a large cluster of these insects swimming together. I peered over at Poker-face and thought I could see a slight tinge of doubt in his eyes, as though the same thought had also occurred to him.

Big Kui was still stomping on the dead bug although he had already smashed it to pieces. I guessed he was trying to get back some of the face he lost earlier when he had gone into a panic. Uncle Three picked up one of the bug's severed legs and gave it a quick sniff. Looking amazed, he said, "This isn't a water beetle—it's a corpse-eating insect."

None of us replied and I felt anything but reassured by this new information. I had no idea what my uncle was talking about but it didn't sound good.

"Hell, these things feed on carrion and you find a shitload of them where there is anything that's dead. The more they eat, the bigger they get. If they're swimming upstream that means there's definitely a site with lots of bodies—and a big site too." Uncle Three looked into the pitch-dark cave.

"Do these things bite?" Big Kui asked in a small voice.

"If this one was a normal size, it wouldn't bite. But when I take a look at the size of what's left of its head, I can't be sure whether it would have attacked with its teeth or not." Uncle Three looked baffled. "This sort of bug usually stays where the dead bodies are and doesn't swim around. Why was there such a large school of them moving together?"

Poker-face turned suddenly toward the deepest part of the cave. "I'm afraid they were fleeing for their lives."

"Huh? Fleeing for their lives?" Big Kui fidgeted. "That means in the cave there must be..."

Poker-face nodded. "I have a feeling that something in the cavern is moving toward us. And I'm pretty sure that thing is gigantic."

CHAPTER FIVE

THE SHADOW IN THE WATER

"Come on, you son of a bitch, don't scare me like that. I may be a big badass but I'm really spooked by that thing. Men on the attack—no problem but this shit? Look at my legs and you can see them shaking…"

We have to leave this place, I thought—something really bad is about to happen. Maybe it was just claustrophobia from the size of the cave that made me feel this way, but I knew I had to get back to daylight.

"I think the most important thing now is to hurry up and get out of here," I said as I tried not to sound like a wimp. "The current is flowing toward the entrance so it will definitely take less time to go back out than it did to come in. I think we're probably only about ten minutes into the cave so getting out fast shouldn't be a problem."

"Yes, yes, Master Three. Your nephew is right," Big Kui backed me eagerly. "Only say one word and we'll all be safe and sound. I promise when we're on our way back home, I'll carry every single thing we have. I'm stout and sturdy. Just a few days—how bad would it be? If I worked faster in the graves we find after this, wouldn't that make up for the time we lose now?"

Uncle Three glanced at Poker-face again and asked,

"What do you think, Menyouping?"

"I'm afraid it's too late to head out now," Poker-face replied calmly. "Now that those two guys have us in here, they're going to make sure that we won't be able to ever leave."

"If we don't try to get out, isn't that the same as just waiting to die here?" Panzi looked at him.

Poker-face returned his stare, then turned away and sat with his eyes closed as if nothing had been said. Panzi saw that he was being ignored and turned to Uncle Three. "I think it's completely crazy to go ahead now. You see Big Kui? He's already scared to death. We just need to turn back and leave. The route we came in on wasn't complicated—we'll find our way back. If somebody comes up with a different plan as we go, we can give it some thought."

"Looks like that's the only solution," Uncle Three nodded. "Panzi, light a lamp both at the front and at the back of this boat, then load those shotguns. Big Kui and I will get on the other boat holding our supplies that faces the entrance and pole us out of here. Panzi and my nephew, guard our backs. Menyouping, you stand in the front."

We all agreed. Panzi raised a lamp and flashed it behind us. The cow on the second boat bellowed when the light hit it and Panzi cursed. "Master Three, we have to throw the cow into the water. Otherwise, you won't be able to move the load with our poles. "

Because the boat we were on faced the inside of the cave, we'd forgotten to think about the boat behind us. Now we felt like suckers. It sure seemed that the scum who led us in here had hatched a careful scheme. The second boat was already taking on a lot of water with the weight of all our equipment, the cart, and the cow. If any of us climbed on, the additional weight would probably sink that boat and everything we had. As it was now, it was like a plug, blocking our escape route.

I could faintly hear that strange voicelike noise again, coming from the deep end of the cave and sounding much closer than before. It sounded like a crowd of little devils whispering secrets that only they could plainly hear, and it made us all uneasy. Everyone quieted down, consumed by tension and uncertainty.

And then I could feel all of my attention being sucked in by this sound. I tried to focus on something else, but was immediately being pulled right back into it. Something is terribly wrong, I thought, this sound is evil, but in a minute my brain was consumed by the sound and I couldn't think at all.

At that moment, a hard kick landed on my back. I lost my balance and fell into the dark water.

Instantly the noise in my head was gone and I saw Panzi plunging into the stream, then Uncle Three, then Big Kui, and last of all Poker-face, holding a lamp. With our heads below the surface of the water, we discovered that the sound had lost its compelling power and we all felt safer, especially since everyone seemed unhurt.

It was hard for me to see underwater; everything was unfocused and shapeless even when I squinted. Poker-face motioned for us to look underwater while he held the lamp, showing us that the stream wasn't very deep and that its bottom was covered with a layer of white sand. He swept the lamp around in a circle but we could see neither plants nor fish. Unable to hold my breath any longer, I stuck my head out of the water to get some oxygen.

Wiping the water from my eyes, I saw a bloody face hanging upside down, watching me with a grim, flat stare. I stared back at him and saw it was our boatman, but only the upper half of him. Where his body ended, a huge black bug gnawed at his intestines. I stood still, petrified. My God! It was obviously one of the corpse-eater bugs. How many dead bodies had it consumed to reach this gigantic size?

As I watched, frozen, Panzi came up to the surface, but he wasn't as lucky as I. Before he knew what was going on, the bug squeaked, abandoned the dead body, flew into the air, and landed directly on top of his head, burying a pincerlike leg right into his scalp.

Panzi was amazing—if I had been in his place, I would have sooner announced my presence to the King of Hell than battle that giant insect. Without a second's hesitation, his left arm moved so quickly that I had no clue that he held his army knife. Stabbing the insect at the base of its leg, Panzi pulled the tentacle from his scalp faster than I could blink as the bug let out a bloodcurdling shriek.

All of this happened in the electro-flash of a struck flint. Panzi hadn't even had time to notice me standing nearby, and that's why he threw the corpse-eater in my direction.

Shit, I thought, how can Panzi do this to me. He had told me how he'd look out for me in an emergency and now that there was one, he threw this fucking monster right in my face. At least he had an army knife, while I only had my bare hands. I knew I'd be finished off right away.

The corpse-eater didn't mess around but immediately

tore a chunk of skin from my face with one of its sharp claws. Gritting my teeth, I gathered my strength to hurl it off, but didn't realize the barbs of its claws were buried in my clothes. A few of them hooked into my flesh, and the pain brought tears to my eyes.

Just then, Poker-face floated up to the surface of the water. He saw that I was almost overcome by the insect's attack, dashed over quickly, and with a swooping motion popped his two long fingers into the insect's back. He pulled and with an explosive force, he yanked out a string of shiny white wormlike things that looked like macaroni. I threw the bug corpse into the boat, and felt that I had just awakened from my worst nightmare.

Big Kui gave a thumbs-up to Poker-face. "Pal, I truly admire your courage and dexterity. You dared to pull the guts out of that monster. I have got to give you credit for that."

"Shit." Panzi's head now sported two bloody holes, which were fortunately not large. He growled, "Go fuck yourself. This is the ganglia of the bug's central nervous system, not its intestines. This guy here paralyzed the bug!"

"Are you saying this bug isn't dead?" Big Kui had his leg already in the boat but hearing this, he plunged back into the water immediately.

Poker-face swung into the boat and kicked the bug to one side. "We can't kill it yet," he told us. "We have to use it in order to get out of this cave."

He flipped the insect onto its back, and embedded in its tail we saw a sealed, hexagonal copper wind chime the size of a fist with engraved incantations covering all six sides. The copper had turned so green that it was a hell of a mess and it was impossible for us to guess when it had been implanted in the corpse-eater.

As Panzi bandaged his bloody head, as skillfully as if he were wounded like this every day of his life, he kicked at the bug and the wind chime moved, making a sound that was identical to the noise that had driven us into the water. But while the sound we heard before was more supernatural, as if it had floated up from hell, now it was much less hypnotic. Evidently this bell was what we had heard, but it needed the open and vast echo from within the cavern to enslave our ears and minds.

What ingenious craftsmanship had made this bell so it could withstand a millennium without breaking or deteriorating? I thought, it's probably made of gold or silver. But how was it able to ring by itself?

The bell continued to chime, as if an uncontainable and bitter spirit locked inside this relic were trying to escape. As Panzi finished tending to his wounds, he grew annoyed by the ringing and kicked the bell aside. Its copper casing had become weak over the centuries; it cracked open when his foot struck it and a stinking green liquid gushed out.

Uncle Three was furious. The only reason he didn't punch Panzi in the head was because the two fresh wounds could make Panzi as easy to destroy as the bell had been. Instead of physical injury he resorted to verbal abuse. "Your goddamn leg better be more well-behaved than that. This thing is an antique and you just destroyed it for me with one kick."

"Master Three, how was I to know the damn thing was so fragile?" Panzi protested. Uncle Three shook his head. Using an army knife he pushed aside the copper debris, and there could be seen many small bells the size and shape of a honeycomb. All these bells were attached on top of a delicate hollow sphere, which was covered with holes. Now that the sphere had been cracked open, we saw a green centipede, its head smashed flat with green liquid squeezed out from its finger-sized body.

Uncle Three turned the hollow sphere with the sharp point of his knife, and discovered a tube coming out of it that was connected to the giant corpse-eater.

"I believe when the centipede was hungry, it would go through this tube to the corpse-eater's stomach to eat," he decided. "How did such a symbiotic system come about?"

The partially devoured body of the boatman stayed afloat on the water, drifting, sinking, and coming back to the top again.

"This is certainly self-inflicted injury," my uncle sighed. "They must have wanted to put us in this carcass cave, wait until we were killed, and then come back to salvage our stuff. But who knew they would find today's misfortune and be killed by this giant corpse-eater. It truly served them right."

"What luck for us," I said.

Panzi shook his head. "I'm afraid that insect wouldn't

have been able to tear a person's body apart in such a short time. If it was that strong, it would have dug out my brains before I could injure it. I think there's probably more than one of these things. This one brought that half of the body over here to eat after the corpse was torn in two."

Big Kui had been looking very relaxed but when he heard this, he choked.

"Don't panic. Didn't our pal here just say we could use this thing to get out of the cave? We'll put this giant corpse-eater at the front of our boat, and let it clear a path for us. This thing ate dead bodies its whole life. Its negative chi is extremely heavy, and can act as a malignant force against any zombies that might be hiding here. I suspect they're probably the supreme chiefs in this carcass cave. If we have this bug on board, we'll definitely make it out," Uncle Three said. "Come on. Let's not give up now. I'd like to have a look at what's here that could create such an enormous insect."

Taking our folding shovels from our luggage in the back, we used them as oars, paddled along the stone walls, and forged farther into the cave. As I paddled, I studied the tunnel wall on my side and asked Uncle Three, "How did our ancestors excavate all of this in ancient times? Even now, it would take at least a few hundred people to dig a cave this deep."

Uncle Three said, "You see how round this cave is? This is an incredibly ancient cave. I think the excavators belonged to a military squad, specifically trained to deter future grave-robbing. It's not going to be easy to find the tomb marked on the map."

"Master Three, how can you be so sure that this tomb is still intact? There's no guarantee that all the things haven't already been looted," Big Kui said. "In my opinion, there's probably not even a cover left on the coffin."

Uncle Three groaned. "If this grave had been robbed by people several thousand years ago, then we're sunk. But you can plainly see that the cave on the map does exist. This means that it was already here when the owner of the grave was buried. This cave has to be older than the grave we're hunting for. And there's probably more than one cave with tombs in this area. Who knows when this particular robbers' tunnel was dug?"

"You mean to say," I already felt the chilling significance of Uncle Three's explanation, "everything we just crossed paths with, including the giant corpse-eater and the hexagonal copper wind chime—and anything that controls them—were possibly here before the Warring States Period?"

Uncle Three shook his head. "I am more concerned about why the owner of this grave wanted to be buried in a place where so many robbers' tunnels were—and why did he position his plot here? Isn't this a huge violation of taboos established by Feng Shui principles?"

Poker-face suddenly waved his hand in a signal for us to hush and pointed straight ahead. There was the deepest part of the cave, glowing with green phosphorescence. Sighing, Uncle Three told us, "We've reached the dumping ground for corpses."

CHAPTER SIX
THE UNBURIED DEAD

We stopped the boat. This was the most dangerous area of the cave, we knew, and we shouldn't venture into it without being fully prepared for anything. Uncle Three glanced at his watch and said, "This type of carcass cave isn't one where we can blithely come and go. In all the years that I've been robbing graves, this is the first time I have ever come across a place like this. I think we've gone right off the map by finding this hellhole."

Panzi cut in, "Shit, Master Three. Tell us something we don't know."

Uncle Three glared at him and continued, "We only know what the old man wanted us to know. Is it true that only the dead boatman could guide us through here safely?" His voice grew serious. "If this really is a carcass cave, then naturally there will be danger ahead. Who knows what we might find as we go farther? Perhaps ghosts will change our course and we will be lost in this cave forever, or maybe hundreds of water demons will come to sink our boat and we will die in this black river."

Big Kui inhaled sharply. "That bad, huh?"

"Anything could happen in a place like this. We haven't even arrived at the grave yet and already we've encountered life-threatening perils. But we're grave robbers, not even the devil can frighten us. If any of you are frightened, go find another job. In our line of work, the bizarre and the terrible are routine occupational hazards."

Uncle Three told Panzi to hand him a double-barreled shotgun from one of the backpacks. "Look at our weapons. We're in a much better position than anyone who came here before us. If there really are water demons here, they're flat out of luck!"

Unconvinced, Big Kui trembled with fear. Staring at his pale, fat face, I said to Uncle Three, "How come your encouraging speech sounds so much like a ghost story? It's not rallying your troops—look at the effect it's having on your man here."

Uncle Three pulled the rifle bolt. "This guy is really an embarrassment to me. I didn't expect him to be such a useless fuckup. He was bragging like a goddamn hero before he got here." Handing the gun to Poker-face, my uncle told him, "This gun holds only two bullets at a time. When those are gone, you'll have to reload. The farther it has to travel, the less power the bullet carries—be sure to choose your target carefully before you fire."

Panzi and I held the double-barreled shotguns. Uncle Three and Big Kui each had their army knives in one hand and folding shovels in the other, which they used to paddle the boat forward. Slowly we punted toward the mass of corpses that were bathed in a dim green glow.

Under the feeble light from our lamps and that mysterious green glimmer, we could see the cave become bigger and bigger. I heard Poker-face mumble words in a language I didn't understand while Panzi cursed vehemently. And then I saw a sight that I will never be able to forget.

At the opening to this part of the cave, the green light showed us that we were entering a supercolossal natural chamber. The canal that we followed became a river, and on sand banks at either side lay many rotting, pale green carcasses. It was impossible to tell whether they had once been men or animals. Rows and rows of skulls were piled neatly in the innermost part of the cave, looking as though they had been stacked carefully by human hands. But the collections of skulls that lay farther outside were less meticulously grouped together, especially near the riverbanks where many of the bodies had not yet completely deteriorated.

All of the carcasses were covered with a thin layer of gray film, as if they had been swaddled tightly with plastic wrap. As we looked, several large corpse-eating bugs erupted from the insides of the bodies. Smaller corpse-eaters scurried over to join the feast but as soon as they arrived, the bigger ones snapped at them and swallowed them in one gulp.

"Look, you guys!" Big Kui pointed toward the wall of the cavern. We turned and saw a crystal coffin, tinged with green, mounted perpendicularly on the cave's wall, looking as if it were floating in midair. Inside seemed to be a woman wearing a white dress, but she was too far away for us to see her clearly.

"There's one on that side too!" Panzi pointed to the other wall. Sure enough—at the same exact spot on the opposite side hung a crystal coffin, but this one was empty.

Uncle Three gasped. "Where did that body go?"

"Could it be a zombie?" asked Big Kui. "Master Three, there couldn't be any zombies in here, could there?"

"Pay attention, all of you. If you see anything moving at all, don't ask questions—just shoot it," said Uncle Three as he stared into the darkness.

At this moment, we went around a bend in the river that took us past a large pile of skulls and bones. Big Kui screamed with fear and fell on the deck of the boat. The rest of us saw a woman with her back turned toward us, long black hair falling past her waist. Her clothing was made of white feathers and the adornment on her outfit I was sure dated back to the Western Zhou dynasty.

I swallowed hard and said, "Here's our missing corpse."

"Stop—stop!" Uncle Three wiped a large film of sweat from his forehead. "Big Kui, take the oldest donkey hoof we have out of the bag—the black one that we brought to ward away zombies and vampires. This is the most amazing zombie I've ever seen and probably that anyone has encountered over the past thousand years. We need our oldest donkey hoof to jam into her mouth and take away her powers if we're going to protect ourselves."

No reply came from Big Kui so my uncle shouted his name again. As we looked for him, we found him lying at our feet, twitching convulsively and foaming at the mouth.

"Panzi, bring me the hoof. Fuck me, if I ever bring that fat idiot with me again, I deserve to have a zombie eat me alive." Uncle Three grabbed the black donkey hoof from Panzi's hands and spat on it, saying, "Take a good look at my skills, nephew. This is a once-in-a-lifetime feat. If I don't succeed, then fire a shot toward the sky for me, so I'll die without remorse."

I pulled him back. "Are you sure you can do this?"

Truthfully, I wasn't very frightened. After all, this was a new situation for me and if I gave it any thought, the sight of a woman dressed in mournful white was more melancholy than terrifying. On the other hand, in horror movies when a long-haired woman in white turns and shows her face, this is never a good thing.

Poker-face drew closer and put his hand on Uncle Three's shoulder. "Black donkey hooves are used for conquering zombies, true—but I'm sure this thing isn't a zombie so your hoof will be useless. Let me handle this." From his bag he took out a long object which I immediately recognized as the antique weapon he had bought from Uncle Three. He opened the cloth scabbard, and inside was an ancient black sword that looked as though it were made of black iron.

Taking out the sword, he drew it across the back of his hand, then stood at the bow of our boat and let his blood drip into the river. When the first droplets hit the surface of the water, all of the corpse-eating bugs crawled out of the bodies as though they had seen a ghost. In a maddened frenzy, they scurried away from our boat. In a second, all the corpse-eaters were gone, leaving not even a shadow behind.

Soon the flow of blood completely covered Poker-face's entire hand, which he pointed toward the woman in white. As we watched in awe, our faces frozen and blank with shock, she knelt before us. "Go—get us out of here—and whatever you do," Poker-face muttered, "don't look back."

6. THE UNBURIED DEAD

Of course I wanted to see the woman's face but dared not risk it after Poker-face's command—what would happen to me if I looked at a mummified countenance? Uncle Three and Panzi rowed our boat with a speed born of terror and desperation. Finally we saw an opening in the cave that looked as though it was the one we had entered earlier.

As we entered the robbers' tunnel, I realized that although I had been forbidden to look back, certainly it would be all right to see what might be behind us from its reflection in the water? I looked and immediately lost my breath. What I saw was the reflection of something clinging to my back. I couldn't help it—I began to turn so I could see what was on my body when something struck the back of my head and I was engulfed in blackness.

CHAPTER SEVEN
HUNDREDS OF HEADS

In a haze, I saw the woman in a white dress with her back turned toward me. Wanting to see her face, I ran in front of her, but once again I could only see her back. No matter how quickly I ran, again and again, I could never be face-to-face with her. How is this possible? I wondered, and then I realized she had no face—her body was made up of two backs with no front. My scream awoke me, and my eyes opened to see the sky illuminated by a bloodred sunset.

"Awake?" Panzi smiled, his face close to mine.

I squinted my eyes to adjust to the fading daylight. Panzi pointed to the sky. "You see that? No shit, we're finally out!"

I touched the back of my head. "Hey fucker, was it you who hit me?"

"I had to. You'd been warned not to look back. You almost killed us, you stupid asshole."

My memory came back in a minute. Terrified, I touched my back abruptly to see if the creature was still there. Panzi laughed. "Relax. It's gone."

"What was it?" I was still lost in fear.

"Menyouping says it was the soul of that woman dressed

in white. She was relying on your positive chi to get her out of the cave. We don't have all the details because he fainted as soon as he told us that much," Uncle Three said as he paddled along the river under the open sky. "But apparently he's had some incredible experiences. Even that zombie knelt down before him. What extraordinary power that guy has!"

I sat up and saw Poker-face leaning against Big Kui, both of them sleeping like two oversized babies. I smiled. Seeing the sky was especially comforting after the dark menace of the cave with its horrible green light. I asked, "Who is that guy anyway?"

Uncle Three shook his head. "I really don't know. I asked my friend in Changsha to recommend an experienced helper and he sent me this fellow. I only know his last name is Zhang so I gave him the nickname Menyouping. I tried to learn more about him on the way here, but all I found out was that he was always either sleeping or lost in a trance. I don't know his story, but the person who sent him to me has an impressive reputation in this business and I can always trust anyone that he recommends."

The more I heard about this person, the more mysterious he became. But since Uncle Three said he didn't know much about him, it was pointless to ask any more questions. I looked ahead into the distance and asked Panzi, "Can you see that village there?"

"Straight ahead."

Uncle Three pointed to the dots of light in the darkness. "It looks like these people aren't poverty-stricken. They have electricity."

A village—I immediately thought of a hot bath, stir-fried meat dishes, and pretty women with their hair in long, fat braids. I began to feel excited. I could see the shadows of people riding mules down the hills behind the village. It looked as though they were coming to the village as well. As we came closer, I began to see that these people did not dress like country people, and I wondered what might bring them to this place.

Our boat pulled in toward the pier and a little village girl cried out as she saw us, "Look! There are ghosts!"

We stood in puzzlement, unable to ask what she meant because she zoomed away immediately. We clambered onto the riverbank. As soon as his feet touched dry land, Big Kui woke up, muttering something about the nightmare he had just dreamed, which earned him cuffs from Uncle Three and a few kicks from Panzi.

Poker-face was bleeding heavily from his wounded hand and remained unconscious. I picked him up to carry him, which was an easy job—his body was as light as a young woman's, as though he had no bones at all.

Uncle Three grabbed a passerby and asked if there were any hotels around. The man looked at us as if we were a bunch of lunatics. "Where do you think you are? Our village has only around thirty families. Why would we have a hotel here? If you're looking for someplace to stay, go to the village guesthouse."

We found the guesthouse. From the outside it looked like a haunted dwelling but inside it was unexpectedly civilized with a phone, electricity, clean sheets, and—best of all—hot water. In this village, it was like finding a five-star hotel.

7. HUNDREDS OF HEADS

We all took a bath and felt terrific after we washed away the stench of corpses. Then we went out and had stir-fry for dinner, even Poker-face, who was finally conscious but with little energy. We fed him a big platter of fried pig liver to replenish the blood he had lost in order to save us. We didn't ask him much, thinking it was better to save our questions until he had recovered his strength.

As I ate, I teased the waitress, "Big Sister, your place isn't so bad! You have concrete floors in here and paved roads outside. Was all this construction material carried by the mules over the mountains?"

"How would that be possible? It would take the mules forever! A highway was built to pass through here a long time ago. Even Mao's Liberation tanks came this way. Then a few years ago a landslide covered up the road and in the debris was found a huge ancient cooking pot. Many people came from all over to have a look and said it was a national treasure that dated back to the Warring States Period. Then they took the pot away because that was all that mattered—they couldn't care less about the road. Doesn't that piss you off? Later we in the village said we could repair it ourselves. But what kind of repairs could we make without funding? Our men worked and stopped, worked and stopped in cycles. It's been over a year, and they're still repairing it."

"Can't you travel by water? Don't you have a pier here?"

"That was built before Liberation and nobody has used it for many years. If someone tells you to travel by water, he probably plans to murder you. You outsiders must be careful; these shoals are very treacherous. For years men have drowned in these waters and none of their bodies have been recovered. When the old people of the village talk secretly among themselves, they say that the bodies must have been swallowed by the God of the Mountains!"

I glanced over at Uncle Three and thought, that goddamn guide that you found was obviously a brigand. Embarrassed by this loss of face, my uncle took a huge gulp of beer to gain some time and then asked, "By the way, do many outsiders come to stay at your magnificent place?'

"Don't look down on my little guesthouse. I can tell you that anybody who has visited from the outside has stayed here. Since the ancient pot was discovered, we've had an increasing number of visitors. There are even people planning to build a villa on the other side of the mountain."

Uncle Three leaped to his feet and yelled, "Hell, they can't be going that far, can they?" He knew, as did we all, that anybody who built a vacation home in these remote and barren hills would have to be either overseas Chinese or grave robbers.

The waitress jumped in shock. Panzi hurriedly pulled Uncle Three back to his chair. "Master Three, you're an old man. Don't get so upset—it's not good for you." Then he said to the waitress, "Don't mind him. He probably just thought it was peculiar."

I heard Uncle Three swearing very quietly; then he forced a smile and asked, "Oh yes. Do you have any monuments or interesting places to visit around here?"

The waitress beamed and suddenly whispered in a

conspiratorial fashion, "You gentlemen don't look like you came to sightsee. Why, of course, you came to rob graves, didn't you?"

None of us said a word as she sat down beside us. "To be honest, what kind of outsiders don't come here to rob graves? If you guys really were tourists, wouldn't all the equipment you carry be way too burdensome?"

Uncle Three looked at me, and poured a glass of beer for the waitress. "Tell us since you know so much, are you also in the business?"

"What? Of course I'm not. I heard from my grandfather that there have been quite a few grave robbers coming here these past few years who took out a lot of good stuff. But my grandfather says that the most important thing is still in the inner part of the place—it's the tomb of a god. The gold and silver jewelry that is easily found inside the cave is nothing when compared to the treasure hidden away in the tomb."

"Oh." Uncle Three was very interested. "So your grandfather has gone in to the cave himself?"

The waitress closed her lips and smiled. "My grandfather heard this from his grandfather. I don't know how far this tale goes back. A celestial god was rumored to have been sent here by the Jade Emperor. He transformed himself into a general, and fought many wars for the king who was ruling at that time. When his mission was successfully completed, his spirit soared back into the heavens, and his body and the weapons he used in battle were buried together in a tomb that is better than that of a king. Of course it had to be—he was after all a celestial god."

"Since this is well-known, there must certainly be a lot of people going to search for this tomb, aren't there?" Uncle Three asked nervously. "Has anyone found it yet?"

"Oh, don't you know? Nobody can reach it now. The year before last during the landslide, that place collapsed into the ruins as well. Guess what fell out of that spot in the mountain?"

"What? Another one of your cooking pots?" Big Kui said.

"Don't be stupid. If it was an ancient pot, it would have been taken away and nobody would ever talk about it again. I'll tell you what, but you can't tell anyone else." The waitress took a generous swig of her beer and muttered, "Hundreds of human heads were dug out of that spot."

CHAPTER EIGHT
THE VALLEY

Uncle Three frowned. "All heads without bodies?"

The waitress said, "Yes! Isn't that creepy? Ever since the landslide, not even mules can make it to that place. If you guys want to go there, you'll have to go on your own. I imagine once you get there, all you'll be able to do is take a look. A few groups of people have been there before and the most experienced of them just shook their heads when they saw the collapsed hillside."

Uncle Three looked at Poker-face, who was slouching lazily as though he hadn't heard a thing. "Before the mountain collapsed, there had to be people who had gone in before, right?" my uncle asked.

"True enough, but I saw them go in for a few days and in the end come back out just as they went in, carrying no new discoveries. They were all happy to leave that place and when they came out, their clothes smelled terrible, like garments worn by beggars. My grandfather said they most likely did not even come close to the tomb. Why do you ask? Do you gentlemen want to try?"

"Having heard what you said, we may as well go take a look. Otherwise, wouldn't this trip be in vain?" Uncle Three smiled, and did not say any more.

The waitress went back into the kitchen and as she left, Panzi said, "Sounds like that big grave would be in the right place. But like this waitress said, it would be difficult to carry our equipment into the hills."

"There are ways to rob with equipment, and ways to rob without them. Graves from the Warring States Period are usually straight pits, going up and down with no coffin chamber. I don't know if this was dug in the same way, but we'll find out when we're at the site. As far as how big the grave is, and how deep it goes, I'm afraid this won't be the same as the ones we've robbed before. The heads that were found after the mountain collapsed sound as though they came out of what our ancestors called a Devil Heads' Pit, a place where humans and animals were sacrificed and then buried along with the deceased." Uncle Three took out the map, and pointed to the circle.

"You see," he said, "this is the place, still far away from the tomb we seek. The people who came before us would have stopped here if they followed the essential principles of Feng Shui. Here is the place we are intended to go. Under normal circumstances, the grave would be right below here. But you see, if you walk farther, here is an entrance like the tip of a calabash. If we don't go in there, it'll be impossible to find out whether there is a different world inside, which is our true goal. The person who designed this cave must have been extremely familiar with the Feng Shui skill of going for the vital point when attacking a dragon, and intentionally placed a decoy spot here for robbers to dig into. I'm sure that below this false entrance is an empty tomb full of intricately designed traps!" Uncle Three saw from the expressions on our faces how excited his speech was making us and he proudly continued. "If it wasn't for this map, we would be stuck here even if our ancestors came to help us. Tomorrow we will take only what is necessary, travel light, and try to go into this place. If it really is in fact impassable, we'll come back to get more equipment."

We nodded, went to our rooms, and began to assemble what we would need to take with us.

We knew we didn't need our traditional Luoyang shovels, choosing instead a shovel used for archaeological excavations, which could be lengthened as necessary by screwing sections of steel pipe to the head. This was easier to carry and much less noticeable than the wooden Luoyang shovel.

Since the graves of the Warring States Period typically went as deep as thirty feet or more, we couldn't pack too little. We each carried one shovel head and ten steel sections to form as long a handle as we might need. Panzi had a short rifle which could hardly be seen when carried under one's shirt. He stuffed this and several rounds of ammunition into his backpack. I had only a digital camera and a small trowel—it was obvious that I was a grave-robbing intern.

Since the night was quiet and my body was exhausted from our adventures, I slept incredibly well and when I woke up, my joints felt numb and weak. We hastily ate breakfast, bought some packaged dry food, and set off on our journey. The waitress was cheerful and asked a kid from her village to lead us to the site of the collapsed mountain.

8. THE VALLEY

We walked for more than two hours when suddenly the kid pointed, announcing, "It's right here!"

Indeed, the valley ahead of us had obviously been carved out by the landslide and we now stood between two mountain ranges. The valley was very long and looked as though during the rainy season it would become the bed of a river. However, having been covered by debris and parched by several months of drought, only a shallow trickle was visible in the middle of the valley.

I patted the kid on the head and said, "Go back home to play and thank your sister for us!"

The kid reached out a hand. "Give me three hundred!"

I was puzzled. The kid didn't say another word but stood with his hand stretched out, his eyes fixed on me. I asked, "What the hell?"

Uncle Three laughed and gave three hundred yuan to the kid. Then he took out a gun, and the boy ran off.

I suddenly realized what happened, and smiled. "The country kids nowadays are such rascals!"

"Men die for birds..." Big Kui misquoted the old saying of "Men die for money, birds die for food." Panzi aimed a kick at him. "Don't you have any culture at all? Die for a bird? You're probably dying for a cock."

We began to climb. The rocks were more stable than we anticipated and we scaled the slope easily. The place was not nearly as scary as the waitress had described, and we saw none of the hundreds of heads she told us about. Behind the collapsed hills was a large canyon which stretched gradually into trees, and then a dense forest touched the horizon. As we stared at the landscape, we saw an old man getting water at the rivulet that ran through the bottom of the canyon where it touched the ruined hills. I looked closely and thought, shit, isn't that the damn guide that led us into the cave? The old man saw us and was so startled that he fell into the stream. Then he crawled back out and ran.

Panzi cursed and laughed. He took out his pistol and fired a shot into the sand right in front of the old man's left leg. The old man jumped with terror and ran in the opposite direction. Panzi fired three consecutive shots, all of which landed right in the old guy's footprints.

Realizing Panzi was playing with him, the old man knew he had nowhere to run and quickly knelt on the ground. He kowtowed to us as we ran towards him. "Gentlemen, please have mercy! I am an old man who has no way out of my poverty. That was why I tried to deceive you as I did. I never thought you would be such supernatural beings. My horizons are much too narrow!"

He burst into tears and Uncle Three asked him, "Why, I see you have plenty of energy. You really can't figure out a way to make an honest living?"

"I won't lie to you. I am very sick. I might seem like I'm in good health, but really I have to take several doses of medicine a day. You see, I am only drawing water to brew my herbal remedy." He pointed to the bucket that lay overturned beside him.

"Let me ask you, you old cheat. How did you disappear so suddenly in the cave?"

"If I tell you, will you promise not to kill me?" the old man begged.

8. THE VALLEY

"Relax. Our society today is governed by law," Uncle Three said. "You'll be forgiven if you truthfully account for your crimes. Only resistance will be treated severely."

"Yes, yes, I'll confess," the old man said. "Actually it was no big deal. The cave might seem like a straight tunnel, but in fact there are many hidden alcoves within. If you don't know they are there, you will never find them. I waited until you were distracted, stood up, and made my way into one of these alcoves. I was supposed to wait for your boat to leave before I came out. Once Donkey Egg heard my whistle, he would pull out a wooden tub, and I would be able to go home. When the mission was successful, the boatman Young Lu would give me my share, which really is never very much." He gasped as something suddenly came to mind. "Oh yes. Where is Lu? He fell into your hands, didn't he?"

Panzi drew his hand across his own throat. "He's already been sent to report to the God of Death."

The old man's face looked empty, and then he slapped his thigh. "He deserved to die. I never wanted any part of this business but Young Lu said if I didn't help him, then he'd do me in. All of you, please understand, I really was tricked into this. Please let me go."

"Save your old breath," Uncle Three said. "Where do you live? Why are you getting water here?"

"I live just over there." The old man pointed to a cave on the edge. "Look at me, I am an old man. I have no land, my son died young, and I don't even have a house to live in. I am just waiting to die. Oh, have pity on me!"

"So you must be very familiar with the area. Perfect! If you want to stay alive, you'll have to take us where we want to go." Uncle Three pointed to the forest.

The old man's face suddenly took on an expression of distress and concern. "My Great Master, I did not know that you have come to rob the grave. You must not rob that tomb—there are monsters inside!"

Once I heard this, I knew immediately it was some kind of trick. This old man knew a thing or two for sure. Uncle Three asked him, "How do you know? Have you seen them?"

"*Aiya!* A few years back I brought a group of people in there. They said they were archaeologists but I knew right away they came to rob the tomb. They were different from other people. The small-time thieves that I'd seen before usually began looting as soon as they saw the graves. But these guys paid no attention to any of the graves on the sides, and demanded to be taken to the valley right away. At that time, I was the only person who had been there, and these people were lavish with their money. They gave me ten large bills without hesitation and I couldn't resist that. I brought them to the woods and took them as far as I had ever been before but they insisted that I take them farther. I refused, and said their ten large bills could not buy my life. They said they would give me ten more, and I said I would not do it for another hundred more. They shook their heads, their expressions changed. One of them took out a gun and pointed it at my head. So I had no choice."

He scratched his head and continued, "Later they stopped and said they were at the right spot. They were so overjoyed, and started pounding the soil with a pestle, saying there was something right below. We found a place to set up our tents and I drank a bit too much that night. Once I fell asleep I was completely unconscious. But guess what? When I woke up, everyone was gone. All their stuff was still there, and the fire had not been put out. I panicked and began to scream but nobody answered. I knew something dreadful must have happened. I thought, since they were no longer around, I could just slip away. So even though I was badly hungover, I ran."

The old man narrowed his eyes as if he was recalling some hideous memory, and said, "I had only run a few steps when I heard someone calling me. I saw a woman from the expedition waving at me and I began to curse and complain about everyone running away so early in the morning. Then suddenly I saw the tree behind her opening its mouth and waving its branches like claws. I looked up into the tree, and hell, dead bodies were hanging all over it. My eyeballs almost bulged out of their sockets and I was so scared I peed my pants. I ran all day and all night before I got back to the village. You see, that was definitely a demon tree. If I hadn't grown up eating human carrion, my soul would have been pulled out of my body by those monsters."

Uncle Three sighed. "You were indeed nourished by corpses!" He waved his hand and in response, Panzi tied the old man up. We could save ourselves a lot of grief in figuring out the lay of the land with this old scoundrel leading the way, and now he couldn't refuse if he wanted to.

According to what the old geezer told us, it would take a day to get to the place where the expedition had disappeared. Big Kui began to clear a pathway, and we marched on. As we walked, we consulted our map, hoping that by using this, along with the old man's guidance, we would reach our destination before nightfall.

We walked for half a day. At first we chatted as we went, but later the vibrant green of the forest created waves of visual restlessness. Things began to look vague and unclear and we yawned without stopping as if we wanted to fall asleep. All of a sudden, the old man stopped.

Panzi cursed and asked, "What game are you playing at now?"

The old man looked at the bushes on the side of the path, his voice shaking, "What...what...is that?"

We turned around and looked. Something was flashing in the thicket of leaves and branches and as we came closer, we saw it was a cell phone.

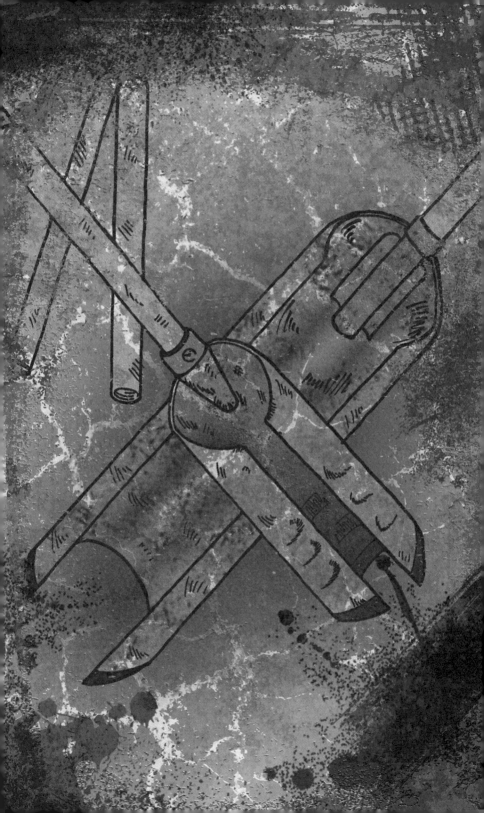

CHAPTER NINE
THE ANCIENT TOMB

That cell phone had obviously been dropped only a short time before, since it was still flashing a signal. When I picked it up, I saw bloodstains on its keyboard and felt less than delighted by my discovery. "This cell phone definitely did not fall from the sky. It appears we're not the only group of people here. And it looks as if someone has been injured."

I opened the cell phone's list of contacts, and saw that the phone numbers were all foreign ones. There were no names with any of the numbers and when I tried to call one of them, there was no reception. Uncle Three said, "Well, we certainly can't go off to find them now, wherever they might be. It's more important to hurry forward."

I glanced around and saw no other trace of people. I had no choice but to continue on the road, but finding such a modern object in this wilderness disturbed me. I asked the old man if anyone besides us had recently entered the forest.

The old man laughed. "There was a group of people here two weeks ago, about a dozen of them, but they still have not come back out yet. This place is really dangerous. It's not too late to turn back now."

"Who cares if we find monsters—let alone whatever devils and demons might be here," Big Kui said. "Tell you what, our young master here made a thousand-year-old zombie kowtow to him. Am I right?" he asked Poker-face, who ignored him as though he were empty air. Rejected, Big Kui fell into a bad mood, but there was nothing he could do about it.

We walked steadily and quietly, reaching our destination by late afternoon, just as the sky began to darken.

There were nearly a dozen military tents, all still intact; although they were covered with rotting leaves, inside they were still very dry and clean, with a lot of useful supplies. We found equipment scattered about, even an electric generator and a few gallons of gasoline. The motor had been wrapped in oilcloth but most of the parts were in bad shape. Big Kui tried to start it up with no success, but at least no water had gotten into the cans of gasoline, so that was still useful.

As I looked at the equipment I saw that all of the labels had been removed—even the trademarks on the tents and backpacks had been torn off. I thought, how strange is this? It looks like these people did not want anybody to know where they had come from.

We made a fire at the campsite and cooked a simple supper. As we ate, the old man looked around warily as though he was afraid that monsters would rush out at any moment and string him up to die on a tree.

Poker-face looked at the map as he ate. He pointed to the spot where there was the drawing of the strange fox face and said, "We're definitely here now."

We all crowded around him as he explained, "This is the place of worship. There ought to be a worship platform beneath the ground where we sit. The items that were buried along with the deceased might be right below us."

Uncle Three squatted, grabbed a handful of soil, put it under his nose, and sniffed. He shook his head, walked a few steps, and grabbed another handful. He said, "If it's here, it's buried too deep for me to be able to detect its presence. We'll have to dig a bit to find out."

We screwed the steel pipes together, connecting them to the shovel heads. Uncle Three stamped a few footprints on the ground to indicate where we should swing our shovels. Big Kui poised the head of his shovel and tapped it into the soil with a short-handled hammer to begin his excavation. As he tapped, Uncle Three touched the metal pipes connected to the shovel head with his hand to get a feel of activity in the place underground. After a total of thirteen taps, Uncle Three suddenly said, "That's it!"

We pulled the shovel up section by section. Big Kui detached the shovel head that had brought a batch of soil to the surface. He came to the edge of the fire so we could all take a look. Uncle Three and I stared, and our faces turned white at the same time. Even Poker-face cried out. The soil looked as though it had been soaked in blood, and a bloodlike liquid dripped onto the ground.

Uncle Three sniffed the dirt and frowned. Both he and I had seen documentaries on zombies, but our knowledge of them was general with no specific details. We could not accurately assess this situation, even with the help of my grandfather's journal. We only knew one thing for sure—since there was wet blood in the soil, the grave beneath us was certainly no small bag of potatoes.

I glanced over at Uncle Three and tried to guess what his decision would be. He gave it some thought, lit a cigarette and said, "We'll talk about this after we dig some more."

Big Kui and Panzi had not stopped digging. Big Kui struck the shovel into the ground a few more times, and then brought it back up to show Uncle Three. Uncle Three smelled every shovel head, and began to connect the excavated holes with lines that he drew with a trowel. In a short time, an approximate outline of the cave was drawn on the ground.

Identifying the position of burial caves was a basic skill of grave-robbing masters. In general, the underground location of the grave was sure to look like the outline drawn above ground. Very few masters of the soil will make a mistake when doing this. But when I saw the contours that outlined the cavern we sought, I didn't feel they were correct. Most of the graves from the Warring States Period had no chambers. This one looked as though there would be one. Moreover, our outline indicated that the roof was built with bricks, which was extremely unusual.

Uncle Three took measurements with his fingers and finally determined the approximate location of the coffin. He said, "There is a tile roof underground. My shovel cannot penetrate its surface. I can only mark the approximate location by rule of thumb. This underground palace is too bizarre. I don't know how thick the bricks are, and we can only break in from the back wall according to my experience. If this doesn't work, we'll have to strike again. Move quickly now!"

My uncle and his men had many years of grave-robbing experience. With fleet movements, their three shovels whipped up and down like small cyclones. In only a minute, they had dug down about twenty-six feet. Because we were in the wilderness, there was no need to be careful about where we put the soil, so we threw it onto the ground as though we were creating a dust storm. Soon, Big Kui shouted from below, "Done!"

He had dug a hole beneath our entry point and had exposed a huge amount of brick wall. We turned on our miner's lamps and pointed them into the hole. Poker-face noticed that Big Kui was preparing to knock on the wall and stopped him by snapping, "Don't touch anything."

Stretching out his two unnaturally long fingers, Poker-face gently touched the surface of the wall, and traced the seams of the bricks for what seemed like a very long time. "There's an antitheft device here," he said. "All the bricks must be shifted outward. We must not push inward, and we must not break any of them!"

Panzi touched the wall and said, "How is it possible to not crack one of these bricks as we work? And how are we going to pull these out?"

Poker-face was busy with a project all his own. Gently he touched one of the bricks and suddenly with an explosive force, he pulled it out from the wall.

I gaped at him. Knowing how sturdy those bricks were, I could not imagine the power it would take to pull one out with just two fingers. This guy was definitely a well-trained and extremely experienced grave robber.

Carefully placing the brick on the ground, he pointed at its back which was covered in a layer of dark red wax. He said, "The inside of this wall is covered with vitriol, an acid used to make pills of immortality. Once broken, this acid would immediately cover our bodies and burn off our skin in an instant."

I gulped, my stomach jolted, and I suddenly thought of the skinless monster my grandfather had seen. Was it possible that it had not been a blood zombie, but perhaps his great-grandfather after a bath in vitriol? Were the shots that grandfather fired aimed at his own father?

Poker-face waited while Big Kui dug a well; then he took a needle and a plastic tube from his bag. Connecting the tube to the needle, he put the other end of the tube into the pit. Panzi lit a match and burned the needle until it was red-hot. Poker-face then carefully poked the needle into the wax wall. Instantly the red acid flowed through the tube into the well.

The dark red color of the wax on the brick wall soon turned white, which indicated that the acid had drained completely from the bricks. Poker-face nodded, said,

"All right!" and we began to move the bricks. Soon there was a hole in the wall big enough for a person to go through. Uncle Three threw a match inside, and by its light, we were able to see inside.

We were now on the north side of the tomb. The floor was made of a solid piece of flagstone engraved with ancient writing and laid out very much like the arrangement of the Eight Diagrams in Chinese mythology. The farther out it went, the bigger its area; the farther in it went, the smaller it became. Surrounding the tomb were eight oil lamps to represent longevity. They of course had gone out since they were in a tomb. In the middle of the tomb stood a mammoth four-legged square vessel with the heavenly bodies engraved on it. On the south side of the tomb, which was directly opposite where we were standing, was a stone coffin and a corridor behind it which looked as though it led down to another place.

Uncle Three popped his head into the tomb to get a whiff. Then he beckoned for us to follow, and we made our way through one by one.

Uncle Three looked at the writing on the flagstone beneath our feet and asked Poker-face, "Take a look at this writing. Can you tell who is buried here?"

The straight-faced chap shook his head and said nothing.

We lit a few more matches, tossed them onto the oil lamps, and the entire tomb blazed into light. For no reason at all, I suddenly remembered the monster Grandfather wrote about in his journal, and seemed to hear the eerie rattling he mentioned repeatedly. My heart froze. Panzi climbed up to look inside the vessel and shouted, "Master Three, there are treasures here!"

We all joined him and saw a desiccated, headless corpse inside the vessel. Its clothing had all rotted away but its body was adorned with jade bracelets. Panzi reached down, took them off the body, and put them on his own wrists.

"This must be the body left behind after the human sacrifice was completed. They decapitated him, offered his head to the heavens, then put the body in here and offered it to the deceased. He was probably a prisoner of war. There would never be any jewelry on a slave's wrists."

With that, Panzi jumped into the vessel to see what else there was to find before Poker-face could stop him. Uncle Three cursed loudly, "You stupid bastard! This vessel holds offerings to the deceased. Do you want to be one of the offerings yourself?"

Panzi laughed. "Master Three, I'm not Big Kui. Don't think you can frighten me that way." He stroked a huge jade vase. "Look! There is so much good stuff down in here. Why don't we turn this vessel over and see if there's more?"

"Quit your nonsense. Come out quickly!" Uncle Three shouted. He saw Poker-face turn white with his eyes fixed on the stone coffin, and my uncle knew at once that something was going terribly wrong.

It was then that I heard the rattling sound that I had imagined just a few minutes before. I turned around and my blood turned to little bits of ice. The sound did not come from the coffin. It was coming from Poker-face.

CHAPTER TEN
THE SHADOW

At first I thought Poker-face was deliberately trying to scare us, but judging by what we had seen of his character so far, he didn't seem like a practical joker. The rattling sound came from him without a pause, but none of us could see his lips move. We all looked at him and shivered. Was it possible that Poker-face was an undercover zombie?

When Uncle Three saw Poker-face's ghostly visage, he pulled Panzi out of the vessel at once. At that point, Poker-face grew quiet and there was a weird silence. Then the top of the coffin flew upward like the top of a jack-in-the-box and shook violently as a ghastly, chilling sound came from inside it. It was a noise much like the one my grandfather had described in his journal—it was like the sound of a frog.

Big Kui was so terror-stricken that he fell flat on his butt. My own legs turned numb and I was ready to plop onto the ground as well. Uncle Three, who had been around and seen a lot, didn't fall although his legs were shaking.

Poker-face turned even more ashen when he heard this sound. Falling to his knees, he kowtowed deeply toward the coffin. As soon as we saw this, we all immediately followed his example, knelt down, and kowtowed as well. He then looked up and began to chant a series of strange words, as if he were casting some sort of spell. Cold sweat rolled down Uncle Three's forehead, and he whispered, "He's not talking to it, is he?"

Finally, the stone coffin stopped shaking. Poker-face kowtowed once more, stood up, and said, "We must leave here before dawn."

Uncle Three wiped his sweat and asked, "Menyouping, were you bargaining with the zombie just now?"

Poker-face made a gesture as if to say, Don't ask. "Do not touch anything in here again. The owner of this coffin is immensely powerful. If he were unleashed from his burial spot, not even God could get us out of here alive."

Panzi still did not understand what Poker-face meant and asked him, smiling, "Ah, come on. What kind of foreign language were you just speaking a moment ago?"

Poker-face ignored him, as usual, and pointed to the tunnel behind the coffin. He said, "Tiptoe past here and whatever you do, do not touch that coffin!"

With Uncle Three leading the way and Poker-face at the end of the line, we turned on our lamps and entered the tunnel behind the coffin. When Big Kui passed the coffin, he pressed his back firmly against the wall to keep as far away from it as possible. It looked very funny, but I wasn't in the mood to laugh.

10. THE SHADOW

The tunnel of the gravesite curved downward. Both sides of it were carved with inscriptions on the rocks. I looked at them and could not make out what they meant. But since I was in the antique book business, and had studied these things quite a bit, I could still understand a few words here and there.

Uncle Three walked very cautiously as he led us forward; each step took a long time. The light from our lamps wasn't very strong and the space before us looked as dark as what we left behind. It was quite a bit like being back in the water cave, and I felt terribly uncomfortable. After half an hour of walking, the tunnel began to curve upward so we knew we had probably gone halfway.

And then we saw a robbers' tunnel and Uncle Three was taken aback. His biggest fear was that some early bird had already caught the worm and he promptly went over to investigate.

As far as we could tell, this robbers' tunnel had been dug recently. Even the soil still had a fresh, newly excavated smell to it. I asked Uncle Three, "The old man said that a group of people came down to the valley two weeks ago. Could they have dug this tunnel?"

"I can't tell. But it was done hastily and carelessly. It's plain that it wasn't dug to enter this place, but rather to get out of it in a hurry! I'm afraid someone else has beaten us to the treasures."

"Don't be discouraged, Master Three. If they really were proficient robbers, they would have exited from the same route they used to enter. It looks to me as though something bad happened. I'm sure the treasures are still untouched," Panzi assured him.

Uncle Three nodded and we walked on. Since someone had already crossed the perimeter before us, we didn't need to be so cautious anymore.

We increased our pace and walked for another fifteen minutes, when we reached a wider corridor. This section was double the width of the first, the decorations more exquisite. It seemed as though we had arrived at the main area of the grave. At the end of the corridor lay a vast jade door. We were sure it had been opened, probably from the other side. Next to the door were two carved statues of hungry ghosts, one of which held an imperial seal. Both of their bodies were entirely black.

Uncle Three inspected the jade door and found that its trap had already been dismantled. We went through the portal. The space was far-reaching inside, and it was exceedingly dark. The glow of the miner's lamps was inadequate for such blackness and could only dimly pierce it, but still we could make out the broad outline of the chamber.

This we knew ought to be the main tomb. Panzi swept his miner's lamp across the room and cried out, "Why are there so many coffins?"

In the absence of a strong light, it was very difficult to see clearly what was inside this tomb. I swept my eyes across the room, and saw many coffins lying in the middle of the tomb. At first glance, I could tell that they were arranged in some sort of order other than the customary formal, neat alignment.

The ceiling was covered with magnificent murals surrounded by square blocks of stone panels that were thickly covered with words. I put my lamp on the ground, and Panzi put his more or less on the same spot directly across me. As our outline had shown us, there were two small rooms on either side of the main tomb, looking like little ears.

Uncle Three and I walked to the first stone coffin. We lit a match, and discovered that this coffin was completely different from the one we saw when we first entered the cave. It was carved with inscriptions and when I took a look, I could actually read some of them.

The text chronicled the life of the deceased in this coffin, identifying him as a marquis who had served under the emperor of the State of Lu. This person was born with a ghost seal which he could use to borrow soldiers from the world of the dead, and so he had never lost a war. He was hailed by the State of Lu as the Ruler of Dead Soldiers.

One day, he asked to see the emperor of the State of Lu, and explained that there was a rebellion in the world of the dead. Since he had borrowed soldiers from this realm, he had to go back to the king of the dead to return the favor and help that sovereign. He needed permission from the emperor of the State of Lu to go back and perform this duty. The emperor of the State of Lu granted his wish and the Ruler of Dead Soldiers knelt down, placed his two hands on the ground in thanks, and died sitting down like a monk.

The emperor of the State of Lu thought he would

return and set up an underground palace for him. He kept the body safe, hoping that the Ruler would continue to fight for him when he came back. The inscription went on and on with elaborate descriptions of the Ruler's many battles. Once he showed his ghost seal, the soldiers from the world of the dead would plunder all the souls of their enemies.

Panzi listened as I translated and sighed, "What power. It was too bad that the Ruler of Dead Soldiers died young. Otherwise the State of Lu would have been the one to unify the six Warring States."

I laughed. "That isn't necessarily true. Our ancestors were really good at exaggerating. If the State of Lu's Ruler of Dead Soldiers could borrow soldiers from the dead of the underworld, then what's-his-name from the State of Qi could rely on heaven's army. I recall there was also a general who could fly. You must have read the Roll of the Mountain and the Sea, right?"

"In any case, now we know whose grave we are robbing. But there are so many coffins here. Which one would be his?" Panzi asked.

I read the inscriptions on a few other coffins which all said more or less the same thing. We counted a total of seven coffins, the same number as the stars in the Big Dipper. None of the coffins contained any clue as to who might be in them. As I was studying some inscription that I didn't understand, Big Kui shouted, "Look guys! This stone coffin has been opened!"

I walked over to have a look. Sure enough, the cover of the coffin was not completely sealed and there were many fresh shaft marks that showed it had recently been pried open. Uncle Three took our crowbar out of the backpack and removed the coffin's cover bit by bit. Then he put the lamp inside to look. Panzi made a strange noise, and glanced at us with a look of confusion. "How come there's a foreigner inside?"

We looked, and not only was there a foreigner in the coffin, but the body was very fresh, looking as though it had been dead for no more than a week. Panzi was about to reach in and dig around for clues but Poker-face grabbed his shoulder, evidently with great force because Panzi screamed.

"Don't move," Poker-face told him, "the owner of the tomb is right under him!"

We looked. There was another corpse beneath the foreigner's body but we couldn't see what it looked like. Uncle Three took out his black donkey's hoof and said, "It's probably something terrible—perhaps a mummy or a zombie. He who strikes first gains the advantage."

At this moment, Big Kui pulled at the back of my shirt and took me aside. Since he was usually quite frank and straightforward, I was worried and asked him what was going on. He pointed at the shadows on the wall opposite the spot where we had placed our miner's lamps and whispered, "Look. This is your shadow, right?"

I snapped, "What, are you afraid of shadows now?"

Big Kui's face looked white and terrified. His lips trembled as I spoke. Impossible, I thought, is he really such a coward? He motioned for me to be silent. Then he pointed to the shadows. "This is mine. This one is

Panzi's. This one is Master Three's. This one is the guy you call Poker-face. Do you see my point? With you, we have only five, correct?"

I nodded. Big Kui pointed at another shadow that stood alone, not near our dark outlines, and asked, sounding as if he were about to cry, "Whose shadow is that?"

CHAPTER ELEVEN
SEVEN COFFINS

I examined the shadow carefully. Its head was bowed at first, then as it was raised, it became huge, and almost wider than its shoulders. My scalp tingled, and I shouted "There's a ghost!"

Everyone turned around and looked at me, but I could not stop shouting. I pointed to the shadow and then turned my head to see what could be casting it—it was a monster with a bulging, oversized head, more terrifying than anything I could imagine. In its hands was a strange weapon that I couldn't identify. Poker-face picked up his miner's lamp so we could all look at this hideous creature more clearly. It was like…like a big crock placed over a man's head…Shit, I thought, as my fear changed into blazing anger, who is this asshole?

It was no monster—just a man whose head was covered with a big crock like a mask. Two holes in the crock revealed two glaring eyes staring at us from within. He held a flashlight in his hand.

I felt stupid for overreacting but we were all still alarmed by the appearance of this person. For a minute we stood staring and then Panzi exploded, "Whoever you are, I'm going to shoot you." As he pulled out his gun, the stranger yelled and ran rapidly toward the tunnel, but Panzi took aim and the crock on the man's head shattered.

"Damn you," the man yelled as he raced into the tunnel, "I'll be back and make you wish you'd never seen me." Running as quickly as though his feet were sliding on oil, he disappeared into the darkness.

Poker-face cursed and muttered, "We can't let him get far into that tunnel. If he touches the stone coffin in there, we're all dead." Picking up the iron sword he had bought from Uncle Three, he raced into the black tunnel.

Panzi wanted to follow him to lend a hand but Uncle Three pulled him back, yelling, "What kind of worthless help could you offer? Go take a look at the two small ear chambers and find out where this fellow came from."

I went to the ear chamber on the right and saw a robbers' tunnel leading from the stone wall. In the corner of the chamber was a brightly burning candle which gave off a green glow. So, I thought, this guy is searching for gold. A bag which he had apparently left behind lay on the ground, and when I opened it I found tools, batteries, and a drawing of a map of the tomb.

Although the map wasn't very legible, I could tell right away that the squares on it represented the seven coffins. There were many notes scrawled on the paper, all written in different handwriting. They seemed to be notes made by several people during a discussion. On the edge of the map was a big question mark, and the words *Seven Deceptive Coffins*.

My muscles tightened. I had seen these words somewhere before. Then I remembered. I had read about them in my grandfather's journal. Of these seven coffins, only one was real. The other six all held traps which were triggered when the coffins were opened.

The dead foreigner whom we had found in the coffin obviously had no idea of the danger and thought all seven of the coffins held treasure. When he opened the wrong one, he was dragged into the coffin and killed. His partner presumably saw this and ran away in terror. Then he probably dug a tunnel in the corridor and fled.

This seemed a logical explanation, and clutching the drawing of the map, I decided to show it to my uncle. But when I came out of the small ear chamber, I found only one lamp flickering in the dark. Uncle Three, Big Kui, and Panzi were all gone!

Going into the other ear chamber, I found nobody. I picked up the miner's lamp and yelled at the top of my lungs, "Uncle Three!"

They would never run away and leave me behind, unless something terrible had happened. There must have been trouble, but I had heard no sound of a scuffle. Big Kui at least would have screamed if there had been a fight or any other sort of danger.

However, the only answer to my call was my own echo. The black tomb, the seven coffins, and the corpse of a foreign stranger were all that were with me. I suddenly remembered that I was not a professional grave robber. It was impossible for me to wait in this tomb. Even if there wasn't an actual monster, my imagination alone would easily scare me to death.

I yelled again, and desperately prayed that someone would answer right away. But all around me was only silence and stillness. The lamp that I held began to flicker as if the battery was losing strength. I began to sweat heavily, as my brain conjured up a series of confusing thoughts.

If this silence had continued, I might have been able to calm myself down. Instead I heard the cover of a stone coffin pop and make a clicking sound. I had no idea which of the seven had made this noise. I started to feel dizzy, and my heart beat so fast I almost threw up my Adam's apple. Retreating to the side of the wall, I saw a flash of light and turned around. The candle in the ear chamber had flared up and burned out.

I sighed and thought, I didn't take anything from you. Why did you have to blow out the light? I turned back to look at the coffins. The corpse inside the coffin that had already been opened was now in a sitting position and so was the foreigner's body, almost as though they had both sat up at the same time. The good news was that neither of them was staring at me.

I dared not look anymore. Closing my eyes, on trembling feet I tiptoed carefully toward the wall. Then I leaped into the ear chamber in as catlike a manner as I was able to manage.

In my grandfather's journal, he discussed his techniques on how to increase flagging courage. His theory was if you couldn't see what frightened you, you could pretend it had never been there. I reckoned he was right. I would never be able to think straight if I kept staring at those corpses sitting upright in their coffins.

I put my lamp on the floor where no light would shine out of the chamber and began to rummage frantically in the bag left behind by the guy Panzi had shot at. All I could find were some broken cookies and some papers covered with drawings and scribbled writing. If the guy had anything important, he had to be carrying it with him.

Other than my dim lamp, there was no other light. In the darkness beyond the chamber, I was unable to see what the corpses were doing—sitting up and down doing abdominal exercises in their coffins, for all I knew. I had no idea and that scared the hell out of me.

Then a gust of wind blew into my chamber from the robbers' tunnel and my brain came to life again. That's right! I said to myself, This cave must go somewhere else and wherever it led, it had to be better than here. I carved a mark on the edge of the chamber, so if Uncle Three came back, he would see it and realize I had gone into the cave. Then I picked up my lamp and the abandoned bag and went off into the darkness.

As I climbed into the cave, I recalled my childhood memories of everything my grandfather had told me, that caves dug in modern times were rectangular as opposed to ancient ones which had a circular form, about the summits in the Qing dynasty versus the slopes in the Han dynasty, about the sex technique of going nine strokes shallow and one stroke deep…Hell, none of this was helpful. As I looked at the robbers' tunnel, I couldn't determine whether it was more circular or rectangular, nor could I figure out when it had been excavated.

I mulled over whether it might have been dug by the fellow with the crock on his head. But if he had dug this crawlway, then when he knocked on the bricks, he would have triggered some sort of trap. And even if he was an expert and knew how to get rid of the vitriol, he would have at least made some kind of noise. But none of us noticed him when he first came near us until his shadow gave him away. So this crawlway had to have been here for a long time, and he must have entered through a tunnel that somehow led him to this one.

Sure enough, after climbing for a while, I saw a fork leading away from this tunnel. It had been dug in a whole other manner, obviously done by a different group of people. Either route must lead to the outer surface, so I could get out regardless of which one I followed. Leaving Uncle Three a sign by drawing a mark on the tunnel that I chose, I crawled in.

I was looking forward to a breath of fresh air and the sight of moonlight. The best part would be to see a cheerful, blazing fire and people above ground who would help me, pull me out of the tunnel, and invite me into their tent. I would have a meal and a good night's sleep and then Uncle Three and everyone else would find me and we would all go home together.

Grave robbing? My ass. I'd had enough. Other guys might rob graves all their lives and bump into one or two unforeseen incidents. This was my first time, and no matter where I went, there were zombies and corpses and insects that feasted on them. I didn't even have time to catch my breath—this was too hard on me! I could only hope that when I found those helpful people above ground, one of them would be a pretty woman who would give me a shoulder massage—I needed it.

My imagination boosted my energy and I picked up

my pace. Soon I could see a fire in the distance ahead of me and I was overjoyed. I crawled up as fast as I could and stuck my head outside the tunnel, eager to inhale some fresh air. Then I looked and my face went blank.

It's quite true that the higher one's hopes, the bigger the disappointment. There was only another tunnel in front of me, and it looked very much like the one I just crawled out of. This tomb was far more complex than I had thought.

I cursed, held my lamp high, and looked around, feeling horrified as I carefully studied the walls. Wasn't this the exact same tunnel where I had come in? It turned out that this robbers' crawlway and the one on the other side were linked, while we had thought this one was an escape route out of the cavern. Why, I thought numbly, had this tunnel been dug at all?

CHAPTER TWELVE
THE DOOR

I remembered that there were some papers with diagrams and sketches of maps in the bag left by that fellow that scared the hell out of us. Perhaps these papers might hold some clues about how to get out of this place. I certainly had no other hope. In front of me there were Seven Deceptive Coffins. Behind me was the monster even Poker-face had to kowtow to. I couldn't go either way; I was safest if I stayed right where I was.

Sitting on the ground, I spread out the papers and skimmed through them. One of them was a blueprint for robbing this grave. Many ideas were written down, especially speculation about the zombie tomb, but the handwriting was so illegible I could barely read it. I could decipher several words about some sort of glass roof and I understood that they had put a lot of effort into figuring out ways of getting past the traps and pitfalls, although it was unclear whether any of these plans had been implemented. Someone had drawn a picture of a treelike object opening its mouth and waving its claws, which also looked like ghostly hands.

I flipped through the pages again and finally saw something significant, an aerial map of the tomb. I saw a tunnel under the water and the place where the Seven Deceptive Coffins lay. The map was drawn very clearly, but the tunnel where we came down was not on it—evidently, these people had not yet found this route. I also saw the cave which I climbed into just now. From the way the subfork was marked, I could see that if I had chosen to go into the other cave, I would have been barred from exiting when I reached the end, where the word *collapse* had been written.

The message was clear—my dream of returning above ground was shattered. I studied the map again, and found something strange and unusual. To the left of the place where I was now standing, where no tunnel could go through, a tomb had been drawn. This tunnel and that tomb were connected by a dotted line, making me think that this tomb seemed to be in another separate area. I touched the wall behind me. Could there be a secret path behind this wall?

Carefully I examined it and refreshed my memories of the construction of stone trapdoors that I had read about in my grandfather's journal. Generally speaking, if this trap could withstand deterioration after a millennium, then it could probably only be blasted open with water and mercury. The trigger of the device had to be a flat board.

The wall near me was filled with inscriptions and statues. If there really was a trapdoor here, one of them

12. THE DOOR

could definitely be moved. But such a piece would be placed on a spot that would hardly be noticeable.

Following this line of thought, I bent down to look at the juncture of the stone wall and the floor. Sure enough, there was a suspicious-looking square piece connected to the floor. I pressed it and although it didn't move, it seemed to dislodge a trifle. I pressed again, but there was still no movement. Thinking I must have been wrong in choosing this tile, I stood up, gave it a slight kick, and heard a rumbling sound.

Then the floor beneath my feet gave way with no warning and my whole body fell into the opening. This was no trapdoor, only a crude trap. I had no idea of what waited at the bottom of the hole I had plunged into but I imagined a steel knife poised to turn my bones into sharpened stakes. I knew I was going to die.

In a flash my butt thumped firmly upon a floor. I was unharmed, but my lamp had gone out as it hit the ground and I was in total darkness.

Losing the light from my lamp could mean losing my life. I reached to see if perhaps the battery had been jarred loose by the fall but when I reached out for the lamp, what I touched in the blackness was an icy-cold hand.

CHAPTER THIRTEEN
02200059.

I screamed, and drew my hand back in revulsion and terror. It was horrible to touch something unexpectedly in this place I knew nothing about, especially because the minute I touched that frigid, swollen hand, I could tell that it belonged to a dead man.

Remembering I still had some matches with me, I lit one quickly and saw a man's body lying on the floor, with a big gaping wound on his stomach. Corpse-eating bugs swarmed around the wound, each one as big as the palm of my hand, and all a light green color. As I looked, I could see smaller corpse-eaters crawling out of the body's mouth and eyes.

I felt sick as I looked at the dead man. He had apparently been dead for about a week, and was doubtless another victim from the group that had left the map. Could he have died here after plummeting through the same trap that I had fallen through?

My match was flickering but in its remaining seconds of illumination, I saw my lamp with its battery lying beside it. Quickly I reinserted the battery and to my great relief the light went back on. Damn, I thought, the guy who sold this to me swore it could withstand a fall of up to ten feet and he wasn't lying. I felt almost happy now that I had my lamp again.

I got up and looked around; there was nothing in this place. It was a square cellar enclosed by walls made of carelessly piled stones. There were many ventlike holes between the rocks, and bursts of cool air blew in through these openings.

Next, I inspected the corpse, a middle-aged man who looked as though he died from the huge hole in his abdomen. He was dressed in camouflage clothing and his pockets were so full that they bulged into little mounds. From one I pulled out a wallet with some money and a railway ticket stub. On his belt buckle I discovered an embossed stamp, engraved with the numbers 02200059. Other than that, there was nothing to prove his identity. I put his wallet into my bag, planning to investigate it further once I had found my way out of this place.

The architectural style here looked much like the tombs from the Western Zhou dynasty and the place I was in looked a bit like an impromptu escape tunnel. I thought it unlikely that anyone would have put a grave right on top of someone else's tomb. This was probably an escape route that the craftsmen of the tomb had built for themselves.

In ancient times, especially during the Warring States Period, if one was to take part in the construction of a noble's tomb, it automatically meant a death sentence. The craftsmen would either be poisoned or buried alive with the dead bodies. But the wisdom of the working class should never be underestimated, and many craftsmen would build themselves a secret passage so they could escape. I swept my lamp across the room and saw a small and narrow door on the wall quite close to the ceiling, just a bit beyond my reach. Below this was a wooden ladder, but it was rotten and had almost completely fallen apart. I estimated the height of the tiny doorway from the ground, and decided I probably couldn't jump that high. And then a face popped in from the tunnel.

Once I saw who it was, my spirits lifted and I called out, "Panzi! It's me!"

Panzi jumped in shock when he saw me, without the slightest sign of happiness. Instead, he looked as if he had seen something terrifying, pulled out his gun and pointed the muzzle directly at me.

What was wrong here? How come Panzi was treating me like a zombie? I shouted, "Panzi, it's me! What the fuck are you doing?"

As if he heard nothing, Panzi fired. The sound of the shot was surprisingly loud in this cave and the bullet came so close to my face that I felt it whistle past my ear. It hit something behind my back and a bubbly gel that smelled like rotten fish splattered all over the back of my head.

Turning quickly, I saw clinging to the wall several large green things that looked like turtles without shells. A few of them had climbed to the ceiling right above me and were only four feet away from my head, getting ready to attack my brain.

Before I could take a few steps back to get as far away as possible from these horrible creatures, two of them launched themselves toward me as though they were propelled by springs, aiming for my face. Two loud bangs announced two more bullets that soared across my head, destroying the two reptiles in midair. My face was covered with gel from the creatures' bodies and Panzi yelled, "I'm almost out of bullets. Why the fuck are you still standing there like an idiot? Get over here now!"

With Panzi protecting me, my mind was much more at ease. I turned and ran. Panzi fired yet another shot at these turtle-like monsters just as I reached the end of the wall. I grabbed his outstretched arm and jumped as he began to pull me up to the tunnel. I hadn't yet reached the top when he extended his pistol-holding arm between my legs and fired another shot. The shell of the bullet landed directly on my crotch and I screamed, almost passing out from the pain, "What the hell? Do you want to castrate me?"

Panzi shouted back at me, "Holy shit! If you have to choose between your dick and your life, don't you think your life is more important?"

I no longer held my lamp; I had dropped it as I climbed and now it was covered with corpse-eaters of all different sizes crawling around the light in a pale green layer. I had no idea where they had all come from and I asked Panzi, "How many bullets do you have left?"

He rummaged around in his pocket and smiled wryly, "Still have one bullet left—for you or for me?" His words were barely out of his mouth when a corpse-eater jumped up into our tunnel, making a creaking sound as it came toward us.

Panzi had once been a soldier and he knew how to deal with this kind of emergency. Holding the barrel of his pistol, he used the wooden butt as a hammer, knocked the insect flat, and kicked it back down below. But more had already reached us. We battered at as many as possible, but a few still climbed onto our bodies and ripped flesh from us with their barbed claws.

"Let's run," I said. "There's simply no way to keep so many of them away from us."

Panzi grimaced. "Where should we run to?" I pointed to the back and said, "There must be a way out here. Look at this tunnel. It had to be built by the craftsmen in the ancient times so they were able to escape death. As long as we run along this tunnel, we're certain to find our way out."

Panzi cursed, "Bullshit. You nerds always think whatever's written in a book is right. Let me tell you. I've scoured all these tunnels for a way out. This is a maze. The fact that I found this place by the skin of my teeth is a miracle to me. If I were to go back out, I don't know how long I would wander around before I got here again."

Perhaps my theory was wrong but there was no time to think of an alternative. More and more insects appeared and I shouted, "It's still better than feeding these things!"

With a sudden rumble, a man fell through the same trap that had snared me, his fat body pressing down on the corpse-eaters, frightening them away for a minute. The unexpected arrival stood up and said, "Damn, my butt hurts! Fuck. What kind of door opens from below?" He took out a flashlight, swept it across the room, and screamed, "Hell! What kind of shit is this? How come there are so many bugs?" We looked and realized this was the guy who had put the crock over his head to scare us in the main tomb.

The corpse-eaters were surrounding us again but this fat guy was certainly efficient. He turned his flashlight into a hammer and struck them one by one. But it did no good—his body was soon covered with them. He let out a hair-raising scream and stretched his arm toward his back, as if he wanted to tear off his skin and all of the insects that were on it.

Panzi suddenly took out every match in his chest pocket, lit them all at once, and jumped down through the hole before I could stop him. He turned a somersault and landed next to the fat guy. The corpse-eaters were afraid of fire and jumped away, but matches are not long-term torches. Besides, Panzi's rapid series of movements had already extinguished most of them.

He shouted, "Do you have any more?" I felt in my chest pocket and found a few, made up my mind, lit them all, and thought, Oh hell, here I go.

Following Panzi's example, I leaped into the opening

and jumped down, clutching my flaming matches. But my skills were far inferior to his, and my body fell forward clumsily. The lit matches in my hand fell, dropping into the pile of corpse-eaters, and Panzi yelled, "My God, are you trying to make me die of anger with what you're doing here?"

I got up and ran to Panzi and the fat stranger. The insects, afraid of the matches, didn't dare to spring at us, but as the flames died down and the glow grew dim, they began to move. I gulped. "Looks like we're screwed."

CHAPTER FOURTEEN
POKER-FACE

The fat guy coughed and said, "Comrades, I've put you into this mess and now it looks as though we're all done for. I've never been afraid of anything but I never expected to die like this."

He was wearing a hooded black jacket like a ninja so it was hard to tell what he looked like, but as I peered into the dark I saw this was a very corpulent man. I had never thought a man this fat could be a grave robber.

Panzi cursed, "Hey fat ass. Where the hell did you come from? God damn it, just let me beat the crap out of you before I die!"

I watched as the matches died rapidly. Close to tears, I begged, "You guys better find a way out fast. Or else it doesn't matter who is beating up who—the insects will be the ones who win."

Panzi looked around and gave the pistol to Fats. Then he handed me the matches and said, "If we'd burned our clothes we could have bought some more time, but any fire made with these matches will be too small to make any difference now. We'd probably be dead before we even get them lit. On the count of three, I'll cover you and distract the bugs while you guys run for your lives to the other side of the wall. One of you climb on top of the other and then pull your helper up—there ought to be enough time. I'll move fast, and when you guys are safely up there, I'll run over and you can yank me up. Let's not waste any more time here!"

Before I could refuse, Panzi jumped into the crowd of corpse-eaters. The insects all rushed toward him like a tsunami, and a clear path appeared before us. I screamed and tried to rescue Panzi, but Fats pulled me back and said, "Up!"

He dragged me along as he ran and with the support of his fat body, I climbed to safety. Then I reached out my hand and pulled him up.

I looked down. Panzi's body was covered with corpse-eaters and he was rolling on the ground screaming in pain. I nearly cried when I saw him like this. Fats yelled down to him, "Quick—climb up here. There are only a few steps to go—hurry up!" But it was impossible for Panzi to climb. Corpse-eaters were crawling into his mouth and each time he tried to stand, he was pushed back onto the ground by the attack power of these insects. He curled his body into a ball, saw us screaming, and shook his head.

His face was completely covered with corpse-eaters, and I saw him stretch out his hand and make the sign of a gun. His arm was torn to shreds and I knew he was telling us to shoot him and make sure we killed him when we did it.

The fat guy couldn't bear to look; he clenched his teeth and yelled, "Brother, forgive me."

The trap suddenly reopened and another person leaped down from above to the spot where Panzi lay in agony. This person did not fall but made a deliberate jump that had him still on his feet when he hit the ground, although the jolt of the fall made him waver slightly. He regained his balance and took a deep breath.

The corpse-eaters were stupefied and began to rattle away in all directions frantically, as if they were doing their best to stay away from this man. Those insects that had come upon us like a tide now retreated like a tide and disappeared into several large holes in the stone walls.

I looked carefully. Wasn't this Poker-face? Fats screamed, "My God! This guy actually survived!" I took a second glance and saw that Poker-face's clothes were torn to shreds and his body was covered with blood, as though he had suffered some serious injuries. In spite of his own state, he picked Panzi up to carry him over to us. We stretched down our arms; I grabbed Panzi, Fats took hold of Poker-face, and we pulled them both up.

It was as if the sea changed into mulberry fields and mulberry fields into the sea. In a desperate predicament we were given a way out. A moment ago we were sure we were going to die, and now the situation was suddenly reversed. We wanted to check Panzi's injuries, but Poker-face waved his hand and

14. POKER-FACE

said, "Come on quick. It's chasing us."

Although I didn't understand what he meant, Fats jumped up immediately as if he knew his meaning all too well. Poker-face carried Panzi on his back while I picked up Panzi's lamp and illuminated the path ahead. Together we ran into the depths of the tunnel.

I did not know how long we ran nor could I tell how many turns we had taken when Poker-face pulled the fat guy to a stop and said, "Okay. There's something quirky about the design of the tunnels at this spot. It should not be able to find us too quickly here." We stopped and I found that I was sweating all over. "What are you talking about?" I asked.

Poker-face sighed without replying and put Panzi down on the ground. I thought, oh right. The most important thing now was to tend to Panzi's wounds.

He was really badly injured; nearly his entire body was covered with wounds. If we bandaged him up, if we only had any bandages, he'd be wrapped up like a mummy. I checked him out. Most of his wounds weren't deep but there were several on his neck and abdomen that could be fatal. Evidently these insects were extremely good at attacking the softest and most delicate parts of the human body.

I remembered the corpse whose hand I had touched earlier. His abdomen was also the most severely wounded part of his body.

Poker-face pressed his hand on Panzi's belly and took out the iron sword that he carried on a belt around his waist. "Help me hold him," he told me.

"What are you going to do?" I asked with a dreadful feeling of foreboding.

He stared at Panzi's stomach like a butcher staring at his victim. He moved his two freakishly long fingers into Panzi's wound and said, "One of the corpse-eaters has crawled into his stomach."

"That can't be..." I looked at him suspiciously. Then I looked at Fats, who was already holding down Panzi's legs and said to me, "Judging by both of you so far, I have more faith in him."

I could only obey and hold down Panzi's hands. Poker-face raised his sword and began to probe at the hole on Panzi's stomach. Then, his lightning-fast fingers stabbed into Panzi's wound, found what they were looking for, hooked onto their quarry, and pulled out a light green corpse-eater. Although all of these motions were extremely fast, they still were painful enough that Panzi curled up his body and thrashed about so violently that I almost couldn't hold him down.

"This just suffocated in his stomach," Poker-face flung the dead insect away. "The wound is already too deep. If it isn't sterilized, it will become infected and that's big trouble."

Fats took the last bullet out of Panzi's gun and said, "Why don't we learn from those advanced lessons taught by the American people, and put this bullet to use? We can pull it apart and use the gunpowder to sterilize his wound."

Panzi grabbed Fat's feet, gritted his teeth in pain,

and yelled, "I wasn't wounded by a bullet! You want to...want to goddamn well blow up my intestines?" He took a bundle of bandages out of his trouser pocket. They were bloodstained and looked as though they were the ones that had been wrapped around his head. "Thank heaven I didn't throw these away," he muttered. "Just wrap me up, and do it tightly and properly. These injuries are nothing!"

Fats said, "Being a hero is out of fashion this year, comrade. I can see your guts. You don't need to put on an act." He began to pull the bullet apart but Poker-face and I stopped him. "Don't be so reckless," I said. "If the gunpowder burns into his internal organs, he'll die instantly. Let's just wrap him up first."

The fat guy listened to me, agreed, and helped us wrap Panzi's wounds. I tore off pieces of my clothing and added another layer of bandages while Panzi almost passed out from the pain. I saw him leaning against the wall, gasping for air, and felt guilty. If I hadn't messed up with the matches, he wouldn't be going through all this now.

Suddenly I was struck by curiosity and asked Fats, "Oh right, who the hell are you?"

He was about to answer when Poker-face motioned for us to shut up. As we fell silent I could hear a terrifying rattling sound coming from the other end of the tunnel.

CHAPTER FIFTEEN
FART

Fats raised the pistol into which he had put back the last bullet, as if signaling to us that if we wanted, he would raise hell. Poker-face raised his hand in disagreement and motioned for us to copy him as he covered his nose. He then covered Panzi's nose with one hand as he turned off the lamp with the other.

We sank into absolute darkness. I could hear only my own rapid heartbeat and the terrifying rattles that surrounded us, All my attention was devoted to that noise as I heard it approaching closer and closer. At the same time, an extremely disgusting stench pervaded the air.

I was so petrified that I almost suffocated. As the noise became more and more distinct, I felt as if I were a death-row inmate waiting to be executed. Suddenly the noise stopped and my heart trembled—could it have found us?

After several minutes, an extremely deep but clear rattle abruptly sounded close by. It was so solid and real—shit, it was almost near the edge of my ear. My scalp instantly tingled, and I pressed my hand tightly over my mouth to keep from screaming.

It was truly intense suffering for the next few minutes. My mind went blank. I had no idea whether death or life waited for us. Another thirty seconds passed, and the noise finally began to move away. I sighed and thought, holy shit, maybe we're going to live. Then a "pop" sound came out of nowhere, and I wondered what son of a bitch would fart at a time like this?

The rattling suddenly disappeared. At the same time, the lamp came back on and I saw a strange, gigantic face in front of me, right at the tip of my nose. Two eyes without pupils stared straight into mine. I was so shocked that I staggered back a few steps while Poker-face shouted, "Run!"

Fats looked clumsy but he was actually very agile. He rolled onto the ground next to Panzi, put him on his back, got to his feet, and began to run. I followed close behind and cursed at him, "You fat fuck. Was it you who farted?"

Fats's face began to flush. "Hell! Which one of your eyes saw me farting?"

Pissed off, I yelled, "I say you're a fucking walking disaster," and Fats screamed, "Ahh..."

Just as I was about to ask him what was up, the ground under my feet suddenly gave way, and I let out a similar cry. Without a lamp we could see nothing in the dark, but we knew what we had been running upon had vanished. And so we fell into what seemed like a bottomless abyss.

The falling sensation was quickly replaced by a pain in my butt. As I recovered from the dizzying plunge into blackness, a flash of light suddenly appeared. Fats had found his flashlight.

I looked around. Here we were, again in another room with walls of stone. It looked very simple and crude, quite similar to the one where we had just battled with the corpse-eating bugs. But because it was a different size, I knew it was definitely a different room. Nervously Fats asked me, "Could this be another trap? We couldn't be extending an invitation for the insects to come and bite us again, could we?"

We have Poker-face, I thought, we don't have to worry about the insects. As I turned and looked, I found he wasn't there. Was it possible that we all had run off in different directions? I hastily recalled my memory and discovered that in all the commotion, I simply didn't pay any attention to whether he was following us or not.

I switched to a different train of thought. We had no idea what that monster was—how could it have let us escape so easily? It must have been because Poker-face had helped us by blocking its pursuit. Had he survived?

As I continued with my thoughts, my heart sank further and I felt worse. If this kept on, we would sooner or later be dead! Fats stared around the room as he put Panzi down in a corner. He sat, rubbed his butt, and said, "Oh yes, I have to ask you this: Did you also come here to look for the royal seal of the commander of the dead?"

"Is there really such a thing?" I asked in bewilderment.

Fats listened carefully for a minute to be sure that nothing was approaching us before he whispered, "What? None of you know about this, and you dared to come down to this grave? Don't you know about the Ghost General and what he did?"

As soon as I heard this, I knew Fats had some valuable information and asked, "Wasn't he just a marquis or one of the minor princes? I heard that his only power was his ability to gather troops from the netherworld to fight with him in battle."

"My ass," Fats looked at me contemptuously. "Listen to me. This so-called Ruler of Dead Soldiers and the so-called troops he borrowed from the world of the dead were all part of a blatant lie. If I didn't tell you the hidden secrets of this ancient grave, you would never be able to guess them no matter how hard you tried."

CHAPTER SIXTEEN
A SMALL GREEN HAND

In my job, I had gained some experience in watching and judging people over the years. I had learned how to assess the quality of the people I dealt with as well as the objects I bought and sold, and I knew that Fats wasn't for real the minute I first saw him. If I wanted to get information out of him, I knew I couldn't be too nice so I reacted as if I did not believe a word that he said. "Like you know what you're talking about. If you really knew, then why would you be in here buzzing around like a confused fly?"

Sure enough, Fats took the bait. He pointed his flashlight at my face and said, "You still don't believe me, kid? Before I came, I put more than a month of preparation into this expedition. Do you guys know what this Ruler of Dead Soldiers did? Or what the whole story was about borrowing troops from the netherworld? And what the royal seal was used for?" My speechlessness put a proud smile on his face. "Let me tell you. This Ruler could be referred to as a general if you wanted to put it nicely. But the truth is he was just like us—a grave robber."

I suddenly remembered that Uncle Three had mentioned the same thing but had no idea how he and this guy knew this. Fats explained, "But his skills were much better than ours—as you can tell by the honor he received when he was given a title from a king for his grave-robbing accomplishments. Records indicate that his troops worked all night and rested during the day. They would often disappear completely and then suddenly materialize in a different place. The places they had been were often filled with "abandoned graves," and when asked about this, the explanation was that the Ruler had used both living soldiers and troops from the world of the dead to fight these battles. They definitely robbed graves everywhere they went, and if the graves that they had worked on were discovered later by other people, they would say the Ruler of Dead Soldiers had "borrowed the spirits" of those who had occupied these graves. This story spread everywhere since people at that time were very superstitious. They believed it was a miracle that spirits of the dead would fight their battles for them."

This story wasn't too credible in my opinion so I asked, "How can you and my uncle form a theory about the importance of this tomb based on this information alone? Haven't you both jumped to a hasty conclusion?"

Fats gave me a sharp look as if he were upset that I interrupted him. He said, "Of course there is more evidence. The most direct evidence is that, according to historical records, the Seven Deceptive Coffins were first invented by some grave robbers. This was because they knew for a fact that many other grave robbers did the same thing they did. They were afraid their own graves would be plundered after their deaths so they created the set of decoy coffins. As far as they were concerned, it wasn't important how elaborate the traps were because mere danger wasn't enough to deter the grave robbers. They had to make the robbers so apprehensive about what deadly tricks they might discover that finally they would be unable to begin robbing in the first place. There is only one real coffin out of the seven. If any of the remaining six were opened by mistake, death was almost certain, because all of them had been installed with either concealed crossbows or black magic. It was not until after the Sung dynasty that some capable masterminds gradually discovered the secret of the Seven Deceptive Coffins. Once the hazards were explained, many people thought it would be an ill-starred venture to attempt to find the one coffin that was safe to open, and the expenses involved in doing this were far too high for most."

Fats was such a sloppy, careless-looking guy that I never guessed he would be so knowledgeable, and I couldn't help but be impressed by what he'd told me. It did not sound like he had finished, so I asked, "Is there any way to tell which coffin is occupied by its owner?"

Fats patted me on the back, pleased by my change of attitude, and proudly continued. "I see you are a studious fellow, young comrade. Well, then I'll follow the steps of Brother Confucius—'Have patience in teaching one's students and don't care about the exhaustion.' Okay, listen closely. There is a way to distinguish the real coffin from the other six. But our line of work has its rules. When they came upon the Seven Deceptive Coffins, most grave robbers would kowtow a few times and respectfully make their way out, so they wouldn't anger our ancestors. But during times of war and chaos, a number of our colleagues had no food and no place to live. Shivering and starving, they had to break their own rules. At that time, there was an expert who found a way to get around the dangers of the six false coffins by using two crowbars to tilt a coffin up from one corner, chiseling a small hole in its bottom, and then fishing inside it with a pothook to see what might become impaled on the point of the hook. That way it was possible to discover what the coffin contained."

I sighed with relief at the information, thinking I should really write a book about the battle of wits between the grave robbers and the trap designers. Fats drew closer and said in mysterious tones, "But I'm afraid the seven stone coffins here are all fake. In fact, I don't even think this grave of the Ruler of Dead Soldiers is real."

He pointed his flashlight toward the spot we had just plunged through to make sure nothing was crawling downward. Then he went on, "Originally I could not entirely understand this stone-tunneled maze, but once we fell into this chamber, I suddenly realized this actually is a tomb of the Western Zhou dynasty."

Surprised, I asked, "So these aren't escape routes dug

by the workmen who built the tomb?"

Unexpectedly, Panzi cursed from the corner. "I told you already. How could this be an escape tunnel? Have you ever seen anyone digging escape tunnels into a maze? Who would have the time or the inclination?" I was greatly confused, as if some argument was forming in my mind but was still elusive. "How could it be possible that someone would put his own grave on top of someone else's grave? According to Feng Shui principles, wouldn't that make that person the last of his clan?"

Fats smiled and said, "You're a grave robber, so naturally you're aware of the teachings of Feng Shui, although those of us who rob graves usually pay little attention to them. Except for some basic guidance to be found in Feng Shui, I really don't see any other use in it. It's a branch of knowledge bequeathed to us by our ancestors which is now irrelevant to the good young people of our socialist society." He made a special effort to pat himself on the chest. "Moreover, this whole thing about burying oneself on top of someone else's tomb also has a name in Feng Shui. It's something called… hm…it's called something like Hidden Dragon Point, or something like that—let's not worry about these superficial names. As long as the numerology is in harmony and the layout is proper, burying oneself on top of another person's grave is not inauspicious. Therefore, the Ruler's coffin is without a doubt to be found in this tomb of the Western Zhou dynasty. I absolutely cannot be wrong!"

16. A SMALL GREEN HAND

Panzi burst out laughing, "What? So you—you moron—you think you actually understand Feng Shui?"

Fats became furious. "What do you mean, 'I think I understand'? If I didn't understand...how would I know so much?"

Panzi laughed loudly, but his laughter tore at his wounds and he clutched his stomach protectively. He said, "I have no idea where you heard all this nonsense. If you really understand Feng Shui, why can't you take us out of this maze? I made at least seven or eight turns and still couldn't find the way."

My short-term memory was coming back as Panzi spoke. I asked, "By the way, when you guys left me behind and ran away, did you know you nearly scared me to death? Where are Uncle Three and Big Kui?"

Panzi straightened up his body with difficulty and said, "I'm not sure myself. When Poker-face began chasing after Fats here and Uncle Three wouldn't let me follow them, I knew something bad was up because Poker-face was so upset. You know, I really don't trust Poker-face. I feel there's something weird about his motive for accompanying us on this expedition and I wanted to try and find out what that might be, so I followed him." He frowned and continued in lowered tones, "I ran for a few minutes and suddenly saw something ahead in the tunnel. I took out my lamp, and then whatever it was vanished, gone like a gust of wind. I got a bit nervous, and walked further along—and then I saw tucked in between the cracks of the stone wall something that looked like a human hand, with its four fingers and thumb all the same length."

Fats looked shocked. His mouth moved a little as if he wanted to say something, but he didn't make a sound.

Panzi continued, "So I went over to check it out. You know my weakness—I can't control my curiosity, I would even eat shit if I really wanted to know what it tasted like. Now when I think about this, I'm still a bit spooked. I didn't expect that handlike thing would attack me. It clasped itself around my neck with enormous strength, so much that I almost choked to death. Luckily I still had my army knife with me. On one hand I was kicking my legs around like crazy; on the other I was doing my best to cut that hand off. Then I discovered the wrist of this hand was frighteningly slender—it was only a bit thicker than one of my fingers and I couldn't understand how the hand could be so strong with only this slight support. I struck at its wrist with my knife and cut open a very long wound. The hand released its grip immediately, and retreated back toward the cracks in the wall." Panzi rubbed his neck and said, "I thought, Holy fuck, there must be something odd behind this wall. So I checked it by knocking it on the left and kicking it on the right. I had no idea what the hell I pressed, but my whole fucking body just fell!" He tapped the wall. "Then you guys know what happened after that. I fell into a stone chamber like this one, and found a tunnel. Lucky I'm still in good shape. I jumped for a long time and finally got up into it—otherwise I really have no idea how or when I would have run into you."

16. A SMALL GREEN HAND

"So you're saying that you don't know the whereabouts of Uncle Three and the other guys?" I sighed. I turned to Fats and asked him, "Hey you fat fuck, how did you fall into that chamber where the corpse-eaters almost ate Panzi alive? You better tell me the truth. Were you the one who provoked that goddamn rattle monster and had it come running after us?"

Fats responded, "Hell, if you really mean what you're saying, then you do me a terrible injustice! When I ran from the guy you call Poker-face, an old guy came out of nowhere and released the monster. Then the man chasing me saw it, said 'oh shit,' turned, and ran. I assessed the situation. If I had to fight that monster, I guessed my chances of winning were nonexistent. But I had to keep going; I hadn't yet finished the task given to me by my team, so I turned and ran too. After I ran for a while, I saw that guy in front of me yelling to stop where I was. I still hadn't figured out what was going on, but he kicked the wall, and I fell before I knew what was happening to me. And I thought following him was going to save me! Shit, there were so many insects down in that place." As he spoke, he looked around as if the corpse-eaters were crawling out to bite him again.

Panzi glanced at me and said, "You see, Poker-face seems to know a lot about this tomb. There are plenty of reasons to be suspicious of him."

I had begun to think that Poker-face was not a bad guy, because whenever he was around, I felt safe, but when Panzi put it this way, I began to realize that all along this quiet bastard seemed to know way too much.

It was as if he could anticipate everything before it happened, and that made me uneasy.

We were silent for some time, and then changed the subject. Fats argued that we couldn't solve anything by just sitting around, and suggested that we go back into the tunnels to test our luck. Panzi agreed with him, so we decided to rest for a little longer and then go on.

I began to doze off and was half-asleep, when I noticed Fats raising his eyebrows and rolling his eyeballs at me. Damn, I thought sleepily, is this guy some kind of schizophrenic? How else could you explain his putting a crock on his head to scare people in an ancient tomb? He was either extremely daring or extremely nuts. Now that one of us is badly hurt and none of us has a clue of where we are, he's still crazy enough to make faces at me. If I had enough energy, I'd get up and beat the hell out of him.

But then I saw Panzi was making the same weird expressions as he stared in my direction. What the hell? I thought, Is psychosis contagious?

Both of them were patting their left shoulders, their mouths moving as if they were saying, "Hand, hand!" and sweat was beginning to run down their foreheads. It was so demented that I took a look at my own hand, but there was nothing wrong with it. Did they mean my shoulder? I slowly peered down and there hanging onto my shoulder was a small green hand.

16. A SMALL GREEN HAND

CHAPTER SEVENTEEN

AN OPENING IN THE CAVE

The fingers and thumb on the hand were all the same length, its wrist was extremely thin, and it looked exactly as Panzi had described—intensely revolting. Fats made a gesture that warned me not to panic but I wasn't afraid. I'd come across so many horrible things recently that I felt as though someone was playing a stupid prank on me. If anything I was pissed off and wanted to bite that disgusting little hand as hard as I could, but somehow logic and reasoning kept me from doing that.

Using Panzi's gun, Fats poked at the hand in attempts to jar it from my shoulder. When the gun came close by, the hand grabbed it, coiled around it like a snake, and began to tug it away but Fats refused to let go. Anchoring himself with his big butt, he embarked upon a tug-of-war with that little hand.

I went to help him and he needed it. Although Fats was very strong, even with my assistance he could barely hold his own against this monstrous little thing. Although he was unable to join us in our struggle, Panzi drew back his arm and threw Fats his army knife.

Fats muttered an obscenity as he caught the knife and quickly cut a large chunk of green tissue from the hand, which released its grasp on the gun, flung itself into the darkness, and disappeared, writhing away from us like a snake. As soon as its force was withdrawn, Fats and I fell backward with our legs in the air.

Fats was on his feet in a second. He ran to see where the hand might have gone and found a deep, trenchlike crevice in the stone wall. He tried to squeeze in but the opening was too small for his bulk. Frustrated, he raised his fists and punched at the wall, which to our surprise, crumbled under the force of his bare hands.

"Look," he cried, "there's a large tunnel leading to a cave!"

We hurried over as Fats illuminated the place with his flashlight. Indeed, there was another pathway within that opening. The interior was very dark, and we had no idea where this tunnel would lead us. Who would ever suspect there was a tunnel hidden in such a dark spot along the wall? No wonder the corpse-eating bugs could come and go as swiftly as ghosts, I realized.

Panzi touched the opening and said, "Looks like this is a man-made tunnel. Could it have been dug for the corpse-eaters to move through?"

"You're saying those damn bugs are in here?" Fats was just about to crawl into the tunnel but stopped when he heard Panzi's next words, "Don't worry. Earlier when Poker-face was taking care of my wounds for me, I wiped some of his blood onto my own hand. You see," he pointed to a bloodstained spot on his palm, "You guys use a bit of spit and wipe some of this on your faces. It's got to have some power."

I could not help laughing. "You're such a crook for God's sake. He saved your life and then you stole his blood!"

Panzi smiled with embarrassment and said, "I don't know why, but when I saw his blood dripping onto the ground, I had a feeling that it shouldn't go to waste."

Fats didn't understand what we were talking about, and asked, "Why? Is this guy's blood that powerful?"

We nodded, and told him about what had happened back in the carcass cave.

"I don't know why this opening was put here," Panzi told us, "but since we're lost in this maze of tunnels, I guess it's our only hope. Why don't we go in and take a look?"

I stared at the opening. Only one person could go through it at a time, and it gave me the creeps. I did not feel good about going in, but if we didn't take some sort of action, we were sure to die in this place so I nodded in agreement. Fats took off his belt and tied it to his leg, saying to Panzi, "You hold onto my belt and I'll lead the way."

Without saying another word, he crawled into the tunnel. Panzi clutched the belt and was pulled inside. I watched them disappear in the darkness, summoned all my courage, and followed them.

Fats slowly led the way. There were a few narrow spots he almost got stuck in and only made it through by holding his breath. Panzi was not only in pain as he was dragged along, but his face was directly in line with Fats's ass. "You'd better not fart right now," he muttered.

Fats was too short of breath to respond, and from his silence, I could tell he was exhausted. The three of us crawled like worms for heaven knows how long. Then Fats suddenly whispered, "I can see light!" He abruptly increased his speed, making Panzi cry "Take it easy!" as the faster pace jostled his wounds. But Fats continued to climb more and more swiftly, which—considering his size—was almost a miracle.

I could see the light myself; it grew brighter as we climbed. I told myself that we just might have lucked out; maybe we'd soon be back above ground.

Fats was already climbing up into the light and the minute he was out, I heard him yell, "Holy shit, where in the hell are we now?"

CHAPTER EIGHTEEN

TREE OF DEATH

I carefully climbed out of the tunnel and found only a small ledge to stand on. It jutted out from a cliff that looked as though it was hundreds of feet high. Gusts of strong wind blew toward us and I had to cling to the wall of the cliff as I checked out our new surroundings.

Like Fats, I had no idea of where the hell we were now. On the side of the cliff was a gigantic natural cave roughly the size of a soccer field. It had a huge crack in its ceiling where just enough moonlight shone through to make the cavern's outline visible.

I was standing near the cave wall to the west.

There was nothing above or below me to support any climbing activity. I glanced around and discovered that surrounding us were many other cave openings, all closely packed together. It looked like there could be tens of thousands of them, making the area look as if it had been swept a few dozen times by many different high-caliber machine guns.

The most amazing thing was a gigantic, towering tree in the middle of the cave that was closest to me. It looked about ten stories high, and probably could not be encircled even if ten men stretched their arms around it. Covering it was a huge number of vines as thick as telephone poles, intertwined and crisscrossed, nearly engulfing everything they touched. Their tendrils hung down like weeping willow branches, some of them swinging in midair, some touching the ground. Other vines extended into the openings of the other caves and spread almost everywhere in my field of vision.

As I looked more closely, I could see many objects hanging from the tree's branches. At first I thought they were fruit, but they were the wrong size and shape for that to be true. Hidden behind a thick, dense layer of vines, they swung as the wind blew.

There was a round stone veranda at the bottom of this cave, leading from a small piece of construction that looked like a worship platform. It stretched all the way to the branches of the mammoth tree, and at the other end I could dimly see another platform. On that had been placed a bed made out of jade, with what looked like a man lying upon it. But it was too far away, and since I could only faintly make out the outlines of what I saw, I dared not reach a conclusion.

Fats was very excited, shouting, "Shit, I've looked everywhere! This must be the main chamber of the Western Zhou dynasty tomb. It's definitely the body of the Ruler of Dead Soldiers lying on top of that jade platform. What a wicked old bastard—a vulture who stole the nest of a dove. He robbed someone's grave and then used that tomb for himself. On behalf of heaven, I'll punish him today for his lack of professional ethics. He'll suffer the fate of any dishonest grave robber!"

Obviously Fats was so upset he was able to overlook his own lack of professional ethics.

Panzi remarked, "You'd better not act too rashly and blindly. This Ruler is beyond anything we could expect to discover. I think there are traps waiting for us in this place. We'd better find a way to get up to the top of the cliff and climb to safe terrain before we do anything else."

I raised my head to look up and was speechless. To climb to the cliff's top would be a horrendous task—especially since we'd have to hang almost upside down as we climbed to safety. We weren't Spiderman—how could we possibly do this?

I turned to ask Fats his opinion but half his body was already hanging off the cliff. Apparently he had not listened to a thing Panzi said. He was agile and swift, and there was no way I could stop him. In a few moments he was already about six feet down the cliff. He was near the opening of another cave and ready to keep going when a hand reached out of the opening and grabbed him by the leg.

Fats began to kick violently in hopes of dislodging the hand. Then from the cave came a man's voice, "Don't move! If you take one more step you'll be dead." It was the voice of Uncle Three, and exultantly I shouted, "Uncle Three, is it you?"

The man sounded surprised as he said, "Nephew. Where the hell did you go? You worried the shit out of me! Are you okay?"

It was indeed Uncle Three. I was relieved, and

exclaimed, "I'm all right, but Panzi is wounded! It's all because of this fat guy!" I stuck my head out, but the cave below was in the blind spot of the protruding ledge I was standing on. I could only see half of Fats's leg, so I gave up. I could hear Fats yelling, "Comrade, could you please let go of my leg?"

Uncle Three cursed loudly, "Where the hell did you come from? God damn it, you better shut up and come down quickly. Be careful where you put your feet and don't touch that vine."

Fats cried, "Which one, do you mean this one?" as he pointed toward a tendril with his toes. Uncle Three screamed, "Don't!" as the vine suddenly rose up into the air like a snake ready to strike, its end opening into the shape of a flower. It looked like a ghost's hand as it waved in midair, following every motion that Fats made. As I watched I realized that the little green hand on my shoulder had actually been the end of a vine like this one.

Fats had the vine moving with him in unison, dancing with it in a teasing arabesque, like an Indian snake charmer playing with a cobra. He's crazy, I thought, no wonder he's all alone. If we let him stick with us, he's going to get us all killed.

Uncle Three was furious, roaring, "I'm asking you, are you done yet? Do you know what you're dealing with? Get down here right now!" But Fats was in trouble. The vine had wound around his leg like a boa constrictor and had nearly dragged him to the edge of the precipice.

Earlier, when we tussled with the smaller handlike vine for control of the pistol, not even Fats and I together could counter the force of just one of these plants. Now Fats was succumbing to the strength of the vine that had him captive, and I had to try to help him.

I began to look for a rock to throw but the shelf we stood upon was without any debris. As I scrabbled about searching for something to use as a missile, I felt the muscles in my leg tighten. Looking down, I cried out, "Shit!" A ghostly green hand had come out of nowhere and had wrapped itself around my leg.

I looked for something to hold onto, but it was too late. A strong force had already pulled me away from safety and my body was hurled into midair.

It felt like I had reached zero gravity. Neither my hands nor my feet could feel anything solid. Then I was flung heavily against the wall of the cliff—it was like being bludgeoned with solid rock. I could feel my heart's blood rise in my throat and I almost vomited up my life. Then I felt the vine increase its force and begin to pull me downward. My hands flailed about but I could find nothing to hold—and then I was in free fall. I closed my eyes. I was finished. There was no way I could survive this.

Three or four other vines had noticed me and rolled toward me from the cliff. One of them was especially thick and wrapped itself around my waist. Hanging in midair, I was like a fried doughnut that had been twisted and wrapped around itself several times. Then the thick vine pulled with a sudden burst of force, my head landed on the cliff wall, and I was dragged along the rocks. I felt the vines pulling me downward as I collided with branches and stones. Not one part of my body escaped the impact of this violent ordeal. My eyes saw tiny pinpoints of light, my brain echoed with agony, and I almost lost consciousness.

When I hazily realized I was no longer moving, I felt extremely nauseated and dizzy. I wanted to open my eyes, but my vision was blurred as if a layer of gauze had covered my face. I took a few deep breaths and slowly gathered my strength as my vision gradually became clearer. I found I was hanging upside down on a branch of the mammoth tree. Below my head lay the stone platform with the mysterious corpse.

I looked again and was stupefied. On the platform lay not just one corpse, but also the body of a young woman beside it. Her corpse was covered with white cloth, her eyes were closed, her face was calm. She looked pretty and charming, with no sign of decay on her body. If I weren't looking closely, I would have thought she was only sleeping. The male body next to her wore a bronze mask that was the face of a fox. Armor enclosed his entire body; both of his hands were placed on his chest; and in them was a box made of purple-enameled gold.

As I stared closely at the corpse in armor, I felt quite uneasy without knowing why. I looked closely at his head and saw through the eyeholes near the top of the mask, two green eyeballs staring at me.

CHAPTER NINETEEN
THE FEMALE CORPSE

The cold, flat stare of those eyes made my hair stand on end. I couldn't stop looking at them as I hung there like a sausage in a butcher shop with no way to escape. All I could do was pray to find a way to free myself.

At least fifteen minutes passed, without the eyeballs rolling or blinking even once, and I began to think this might just be an illusion. But the strange eyes kept staring right into mine; even if they had been the eyes of a god, that would have been bound to make me uncomfortable.

I looked away and thought, I'd better come up with a way out quick. If I continue hanging upside down like this, my brain will sooner or later burst from all of my blood flowing into it.

Using all of my remaining strength, I raised my head and found I was almost completely covered with bruises and my legs were ensnared by a vine. I turned around, and almost vomited—all around me as far as I could see were corpses hanging from the branches of the tree. It looked as though there were tens of thousands of them, swaying in the wind, like a wind chime made up of human bones.

There were human bodies and animal carcasses too. Most of them were dry bones but some were still rotting and stunk terribly. Corpse-eaters of all sizes crowded together like mosquitoes, nibbling on the decomposing bodies. I was grateful I had wiped some of Poker-face's blood from Panzi's body onto my own, since that seemed to be keeping them away from me. Although I felt guilty for taking somebody else's blood, guilt was still better than losing my shoulder or leg.

Suddenly I remembered that, like me, Fats had also been captured, and I began to worry about him. But when I looked about, it was hard to see through the vines that surrounded me. I searched my pockets but all I had with me was my digital camera, which was of no use in this predicament.

As I felt annoyed and upset with myself, the vine around my legs suddenly loosened. My entire body sank downward, and I thought I was about to fall to my death. I covered my head with my arms for protection but discovered the vine had only loosened a trifle.

When I opened my eyes, I saw that I was almost face-to-face with the female corpse. If I fell just a little farther, our lips would touch. I pulled my neck back with all of my might and tucked my lips into my mouth so it would be impossible for me to kiss the dead woman. Then suddenly I caught sight of a small dagger attached to the waist of the armored man that lay beside her. My heart lightened and I whispered, "My fair lady, I am now compelled by this situation to ask your friend if I can borrow his knife. I hope he won't mind?"

I twisted my waist and stretched my arm out towards the dagger with every ounce of my strength. After swinging back and forth several times, my hand caught the dagger's handle. I pulled it with all the force I could muster; the knife was attached so tightly that I pulled off the belt that held it and all of its contents.

Shit! I thought, Now that I've stolen his belt, this corpse is bound to turn hostile if he has any power at all. I quickly clamped onto the belt with both legs and pulled out the dagger with all of my might. The blade flashed, letting me know at once that this was a fine weapon and a gift from the heavens. Quickly I cut away the vines that bound me to the tree branch, without thinking what my liberated body might fall upon. With no time to regret my lack of forethought, in only the fraction of a second, my whole body landed on top of the female corpse.

To be honest, I was lucky to have held my breath when I fell so I didn't land with the pressure of my full weight. Otherwise I'm sure that my bulk would have pressed ancient feces from the woman's body. But even so, there was no distance between my body and hers; my mouth was directly on her dead lips in the kiss I had feared only seconds before, and chills racked my spine.

As I lay as still as a wooden statue, I thought of her tongue entering my mouth and going straight down my throat to suck out all my internal organs. I supposed I should be grateful that I was kissing the corpse of a beautiful woman—if she had been a man I would be dead from disgust by now.

Time passed with no tongue issuing from her mouth and I thought, my luck hasn't run out yet. At last I've met a merciful tomb inhabitant. Slowly I lifted up my head and began to move it slowly away from the dead woman. My head was raised only halfway when a stream of fragrance burst into the air and the female corpse's arms wrapped around my neck in a firm embrace.

I was petrified; my whole body froze. The armored corpse beside her began to make a rattling noise and I knew I was in trouble. I yelled silently, "Brother, don't get me wrong—it's your wife who's hitting on *me*."

Turning my head, I saw the sound had come from a piece of armor that fell from the belt I had just taken from the male corpse. That was a relief—as was my grateful realization that it was the female corpse that had her arms around me instead of the monster next to her. Otherwise I would certainly have pissed myself.

The ghastly embrace lasted for over ten seconds. When I saw that the female corpse had not made any other moves on me, I began to stealthily move my head out from under her arms. But when I moved, her arms moved with me, following my every move—when I leaned forward, she leaned forward; and when I moved backward, she did the same.

I thought I could break free by simply lifting my head and sliding away with a somersault. But I hadn't realized how tightly her arms were wrapped around my neck, and when I raised my head, I ended up pulling her to a seated position. With the jolt of this motion, the lips of the female corpse parted, revealing something inside her mouth.

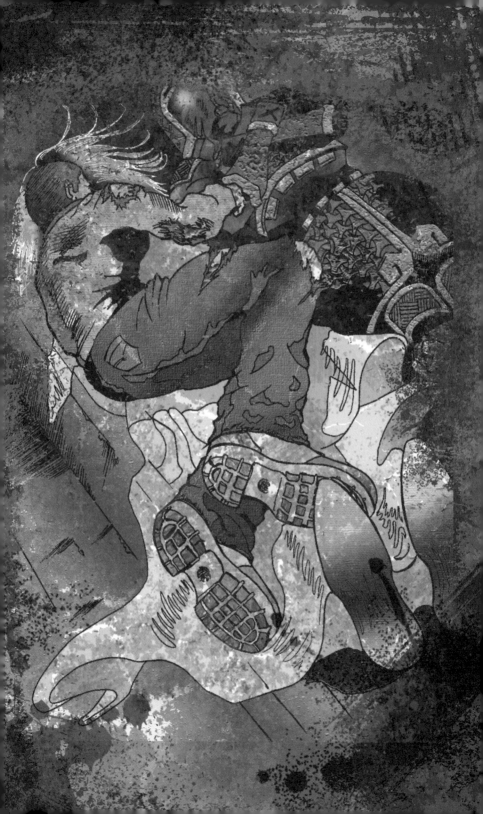

CHAPTER TWENTY

THE KEY

In the mouth of this lovely corpse was what seemed to be a copper key inset with an extraordinary dark green pearl. I wasn't completely sure that was what the jewel was, but I knew that sometimes our ancestors put pearls into the mouths of the dead as a way to prevent corruption. If I removed this key, this thousand-year-old dead beauty might instantly turn into a mummy before my eyes.

I didn't have the courage to do such a terrifying thing, yet my present situation was rather awkward. I was imprisoned in a dead woman's embrace, and there was no way I could carry her with me and run to safety at the same time.

As I was hesitating over what to do next, I suddenly heard someone shouting from above me. I looked up and saw a man, hanging upside down and yelling as he struggled with seven or eight branches at the same time. It was that goddamn Fats, looking as though he was ready to give up. He was even more bruised than I was, although he didn't appear to have collided with the cliff wall in his descent.

He cursed to himself, "Fuck, I didn't expect these cock-sucking branches to have such tremendous strength!" Then he caught sight of me and said, "Little comrade, what are you doing to that pretty girl?"

I didn't know whether to laugh or scream. But I didn't dare speak too loudly, so I muttered to Fats, "Fuck you—she's dead. Help me think of something quickly!"

"Ah!" Fats exhaled; he wiggled his butt in midair and said, "But I still have to come down first!" I threw the dagger in my hand upward and he caught it, turned, and immediately began to cut away the vines. At first I did not realize the mistake he was making, and when I did it was already too late.

Before I could tell him to wait a minute, Fats fell right on top of the armored corpse, knocking off his mask. I was about to poke up my head to take a look when Fats shouted, "Don't look. This is a green-eyed fox-corpse!"

His warning came too late. I had already seen the face that had been concealed by the mask. My brain buzzed and my body was awash with goose bumps. I stammered, "How could that ever have been a man?"

Under the mask was a piercingly white face. As I looked carefully, I could only faintly see where its nose and mouth had once been. There was no hair anywhere on its head. Even its eyebrows were gone. The shape of its face was so pointed it was deformed, with eyes that had become only two narrow slits that glowed with a green light.

The face really did look like a foxlike human with a malignant smile. Its strangest features were those two green eyeballs, which were so truly horrifying that I dared not look into them directly. I was becoming accustomed to seeing corpses but this creature was capable of scaring me to death with his gaze.

Fats was terrified as well. He rolled off the jade platform as quickly as he could, saying in amazement, "I can't believe it! How can the Ruler of Dead Soldiers actually look so hideously disgusting!"

"Is this really the Ruler?" I asked. "How come he looks like…like a fox?"

As his eyes wandered up and down the armored corpse, Fats replied, "I had a friend who once told me that this sort of creature is called a green-eyed fox-corpse. A long time ago, a man robbed a grave from an unknown dynasty. When he opened the cover of the coffin, he found a green-eyed fox lying on top of the corpse. The fox was a demon, and it was a bad omen that it was lying there. The rule was that everything in the grave was supposed to remain intact and in place, but the grave robber was inexperienced and took a jade turtle away with him when he left. Some years later, he quit this career and returned to his village to marry the woman who waited for him there. His wife got pregnant, and during her delivery, the midwife screamed and fainted. The man rushed to the bedside and saw that their newborn baby had a pair of long, squinty green eyes. The man at first did not realize it was the fox demon at work. He merely thought the child had a strange disease, and searched everywhere for doctors who could cure it. The child's sickness not only became worse, but his hair began to fall out and his face also began to look more and more like that of a fox. It was only then that the grave robber realized what had caused this misfortune, so he made a long and difficult journey back to the ancient tomb and put the jade turtle back in the coffin. From then on, the child's sickness got no worse but his strange, foxlike face never went away."

Fats sighed and said, "The eyes of this green-eyed fox-corpse are very powerful. I've heard that if you give him one look, your face will eventually become like his. Did you look at him a minute ago?"

Although I did not completely believe it, hearing that my face might turn the same as this monster's made me shiver. "Stop talking nonsense! Whether my face will change or not isn't the problem," I shouted. "Just help me get out of this dead woman's arms before you say another word!"

Fats realized it was foolish for him to babble on like this and he began to try to release me. He tried to break the corpse's grip, but her arms were as immovable as if they were made of iron and he only ended up panting with exhaustion.

Seeing the worried look in my eyes he said to me in a comforting tone, "Don't worry. I have plenty of tricks. If this doesn't work, I can always cut off her arms."

I screamed, "No way! What if there's poison inside her body? You can't do that. Besides, I don't have a grain of hatred for her. To cut her arms off at first meeting would be too uncivilized and merciless."

Fats shook his head. There was no other solution.

He said to me, "Generally speaking, when a dead body remains soft and flexible, it harbors unfulfilled wishes. If you help her get her wish, she will let you go. Why don't you think now—a moment ago when she hooked her arms around you, did anything unusual happen?"

Then I remembered that when I first raised my head, her mouth had suddenly fallen open, revealing something that looked like a key inside it. Perhaps this was a clue to the woman's unfulfilled wish. Very gently I moved the female corpse's head upright, and softly whispered, "Forgive my offense!" Then I pressed her cheeks; her apricot-colored lips parted and her mouth opened. There under her tongue was the copper key inlaid with a pearl.

Fats gasped with surprise. "Shit, this is great! She must certainly want you to take that key out. You see how small her mouth is? It must be really uncomfortable to hold a key in there."

Anxiously I asked, "If she bites me, what will I do?"

Fats replied impatiently, "Do you see how many vulnerable spots you have all over your body? She could bite you anytime and anywhere she wants. Why would she want to bite your hand?"

He had a point, and I told myself that it wouldn't be such a big deal to lose a finger or two anyway. So I took a deep breath, and began to stretch my two trembling fingers towards her mouth. When I had almost reached her lips, a voice beside my ear said, "Stop."

CHAPTER TWENTY-ONE
THE GREEN-EYED
FOX-CORPSE

My God, I thought, that's Uncle Three's voice, but isn't he still up on the cliff? How could he sound so close to me? Turning around to look for him, I saw only Fats—nobody else was there. Then I heard Uncle Three again. "Your hand is warm and alive now but the minute you put it in that corpse's mouth, you'll be dead meat. Don't be so stupid."

I listened hard to find the source of the voice—it seemed to be coming from under the jade platform and baffled, I asked, "Uncle Three, how did you get beneath this platform?"

"I'll explain to you later," my uncle's voice replied. "Just now, do as I tell you—lower the woman's head, press your thumb against her throat, and then hit her on the back of the head once. Remember to push on her throat with your thumb or she'll swallow the key." I nodded and obeyed, pressing on the throat of the female corpse and lightly striking the back of her head. The key flew out of her mouth, landing on the jade platform.

I immediately felt my shoulders relax as the arms of the female corpse fell away from me and her body lay flat on the platform. I let out a long sigh of relief as I realized I had been released from the dead woman's embrace. Then I heard Uncle Three speaking from below, "Nephew, is Fats still next to you?"

I lifted my head and saw that Fats had already picked up the key and was inspecting it carefully. "Yes, he is," I nodded.

"Take a look," Uncle Three said in the Hangzhou dialect, "and tell me if he casts a shadow."

I didn't understand what my uncle meant. Obediently I glanced sideways at Fats's feet but saw only the jade bed where his shadow should have been. Without raising my head, I was unable to see if his shadow was visible or not. "I can't see him clearly right now," I said.

Uncle Three sounded agitated as he told me, "Listen to me. I'll tell you something—don't be scared. On the way here just now, I looked closely at that guy's body. You have to be careful. Fats is not human."

I glanced at Fats and noticed his pink and ruddy complexion. Judging by the way he looked and the way he moved, it seemed impossible for him to be a ghost. "Uncle Three," I asked, "could you have seen someone else instead?"

"No, it was definitely him," my uncle assured me, "I'm not mistaken. Didn't he urge you to put your hand into the female corpse's mouth just now? He was trying to kill you."

In a panic, I blurted out, "So you're saying Fats is a ghost?"

Uncle Three answered, "Yes. No matter what he

says, don't believe him. Now, be quick! Find something nearby to protect yourself against the evil that he plans to do to you."

At this moment, Fats gave me a look that held both anger and resentment, making me believe at least half of what my uncle claimed was true. I felt around nervously and found the belt that I had pulled from the waist of the armored corpse. Guessing that our ancestors carved spells on their belts to protect themselves from evil, I grabbed it.

Although the words on the belt were badly faded, I could still identify the text as that of the State of Lu. Could this corpse really be the Ruler of Dead Soldiers? Was this woman next to him his wife?

As these thoughts ran through my mind, my eyes were working overtime. I had already scanned the text once and although I didn't understand most of it, there were a few words I easily recognized. Traced in gold powder, they said *The Ruler of Yinxi*—the king of the western underworld—this was indeed a spell to ward off evil spirits. I was delighted.

A disturbing question popped into my head and I asked Uncle Three, "Something's not right. This jade bed isn't transparent. How can you see us?"

"I don't know," my uncle told me, "I can see you clearly from below, as if the bed were made of window glass. When I came to this spot, you were just about to put your hand into the female corpse's mouth to take the key. So I yelled out to stop you, and luckily you could hear me. Otherwise, it would have been terrible if you had put your hand between her jaws."

I was even more confused, and still felt something was wrong. This jade bed was quite narrow and the two corpses on it were jammed close together, covering the entire bed. What's more, the moon beams weren't particularly bright. To be able to see through two corpses so clearly under such a small amount of moonlight seemed highly improbable, even if the bed was somehow transparent.

I glanced over at Fats again and saw that he was still examining the key. Suddenly I was sure something was askew.

Fats was the kind of guy who would have interrupted my uncle's speech, even if he did not understand the Hangzhou dialect that Uncle Three was using. And it was completely out of character for Fats to sit still for so long staring at a key in silence.

I got off the jade bed and patted his beefy shoulder to see how Fats would respond, but to my shock, his reaction was completely out of control. Staring at me in fury, he bellowed, "You goddamn kid—you've been lying to me all this time!" Raising his hand that still held the dagger I had thrown to him, he began to stab in my direction.

Taking several steps backward, I screamed, "What the hell are you doing?"

His eyes were bloodred and he didn't seem to be able to hear me. Rushing towards me, he tried to stab me again. His movements were precise and forceful, and I figured if I didn't run, I was going to get hurt. I raced down the steps, with Fats behind me. "It's no good to run from me, you bastard," he roared, grinding his teeth with rage as if I had just murdered his father. I ran for my life. Fats had a gross and bloated body, but he could move like an Olympic racer. The tunnel I was following was a short one and in a second I would be at the end of the burial platform. Behind that, the area was filled with vines. If I stepped on one, I would again soon be hanging upside down like a sausage.

Could Fats really be a devil, intending to pull me down into hell and make me suffer? But what kind of devil ran about the earth stabbing people with a knife?

As my thoughts wandered, the tunnel before me ended. I halted abruptly and lashed the belt in my hand towards Fats as though I were wielding a whip. He dodged away and I charged over to bite his hand that clutched the dagger, thinking, I'm probably the first person in the world who dared to bite the hand of a ghost. Fats screamed in pain. The dagger dropped to the ground and I kicked it far out of reach.

Fats grabbed me, threw me to the ground and muttered, "I'll fucking strangle you, you son of a bitch," as he put me in a headlock. I wrapped the belt around his neck, thinking, Play dirty, will you, fat man—I can do that too.

I pulled tightly on the belt and he pressed his grip tightly around my neck, each of us desperately trying to strangle the other before we were suffocated ourselves. Fats was fighting to the death, choking me so viciously that I almost bit off my tongue. Repaying him in kind, I used all the strength I had. But the belt which looked so well-preserved was weak with age. As I pulled on it, it popped and broke into two pieces.

The leather that the belt was made of was ornamented with pieces of copper that flew all over the place when the belt broke in two. The piece of copper engraved with the words *The Ruler of Yinxi* landed straight in my mouth and I felt a bitter liquid roll down my throat. Knowing that the piece had recently been on a dead body, I choked with nausea and a cloud of mist appeared before my eyes as if I had fallen into a thick, black fog.

What's happened to me? I wondered, could Fats have choked me to death so quickly? The taste of bitterness grew stronger and stronger in my mouth. The cloud before my eyes turned clearer by the second and I woke up with a start to find that I was pressed down on the jade bed. Fats had his hands tightly around my neck, his arms were tightly hooked around my shoulders, and his eyes had turned to a shade of brilliant green.

The copper key with the dark green pearl was still inside the female corpse's mouth, and her arms still tightly embraced me. Suddenly I realized that during the past few minutes I had been under the power of an illusion.

Turning my head, I looked at the green-eyed fox-corpse. His mask was still on the ground and the two eyeballs inside his narrow sockets had rolled in our direction as he stared straight at us.

I thought to myself, Shit! No wonder Fats had told me earlier not to look at this—the green eyes of that fox-corpse had a dreadful power. Fats was still strangling me with enormous strength and if that copper piece had ever really been in my mouth, it had by now completely dissolved. Suddenly from the corner of my eye I spotted the purple-enameled gold box in the hands of the fox-corpse. Stretching out my arm, I grabbed it and hit Fats on the head with it as hard as I could.

Fats never loosened his grip—if anything he held on to my neck tighter than ever. You plan to choke me to death and rip my neck from my body, I thought, and I knew I had to stop this guy somehow, so I hit him again even harder than before. Then there was a strange sound, Fats's eyes rolled back into his head, and he fell forward onto my body, releasing his stranglehold on my throat. Coughing up blood, I suddenly saw the green eyes of the fox-corpse open wide and staring in Fats's direction, emitting a surge of power that forced me to look into them.

I felt as though I was again losing control of my mind—there was nothing for me to do but push Fats on top of the corpse, since I no longer cared for him very much at all. His huge body completely covered the corpse and since I could no longer see that dreadful green-eyed stare, I began to regain my mental equilibrium.

I rubbed my neck, which was bruised with huge fingerprints and so swollen that its shape was distorted. My whole body hurt. The powerful hypnotic stare of that green-eyed fox- corpse was not to be underestimated.

Picking up the purple-enameled gold box I had just used as a weapon, I found it had a tiny keyhole. "Hmm," I grunted and looked over at the female corpse's mouth, as I muttered to myself, "Could that key open this box?" And then I saw the corpse's belt, torn in two, with little bits of copper scattered everywhere. Suddenly the memory of the taste of copper filled my mouth like blood.

CHAPTER TWENTY-TWO

DISINTEGRATION OF A BEAUTIFUL CORPSE

The box felt heavy and looked like the ones that contained Buddhist relics. But at the time this box was made, Buddhism had not yet come to China, so whatever was inside couldn't be a sacred relic. I shook my head as I asked myself, Could the devil's imperial seal that Fats talked about earlier be inside this box?

The key was still in the female corpse's mouth. I pulled myself together, reached under her tongue with two fingers, grabbed the key, and carefully began to remove it. When the key was halfway out, I noticed a very fine string of silk thread tied to it that went all the way down the dead woman's throat. The end of this thread seemed to be tied to something and I realized this could be a very bad sign.

Grandfather had told me that ingenious Chinese craftsmen of the Shang dynasty were able to place crossbows inside a dead body which were usually triggered by pulling a gold thread. Once a grave robber removed the jade or the pearls that had been concealed within a corpse's mouth or asshole, the motion would tug the thread that triggered the trap, and bolts would shoot out of the corpse. Because the distance between the robber and the dead body was usually very close when this happened, it was impossible to avoid the attack. Heaven knew how many grave robbers died from this trap, but I didn't want to be one of them.

Pressing the stomach of the dead woman, I felt some hard objects under her skin. Lucky that I'm such a slow and cautious guy, I thought. If Fats or Panzi were doing this, by now they would most likely have been fooled and killed by this trap designed to kill grave robbers like us. I shivered with fear and relief.

The thread tied to the key was made of gold; it could be pulled but not twisted. I pinched it with my fingernails until I broke it, and cautiously removing the key, I inserted it in the keyhole of the box. It fit perfectly.

But was there anything dangerous inside the box? There could well be other traps so I decided it was best to keep it locked for now.

Suddenly I felt a ferocious intensity coming from the female corpse. Her embracing arms fell from my shoulders at last. Her face instantly caved in upon itself, like a rotting orange. An indescribable noise came from her throat that made me clap my hands over my ears. As I shivered in disbelieving horror, the perfect beauty in front of me became a mummified corpse. Her withered, putrefied body fell onto the jade platform, shrinking and becoming smaller by the second.

It was an appalling spectacle. Evidently the pearl on the key had prevented her from rotting over the past centuries. I stuffed the box and its key into my bag, thinking I'd spent too much time already in this place. Then I went to find Fats.

He was pretty battered from our fight and didn't move even when I made several attempts to pull him to his feet. He can't be that bad off, I told myself. I certainly hadn't beaten him to death—not that I would have cared if I had. I grabbed him by the arm, yelled "Up!" and slung him over my back.

Fats was deadweight and of course extremely heavy. His bulk pressed into me as I spat out blood from our fight. I shook my head and cursed his ancestors as I walked with his corpulence burdening my shoulders.

Fortunately the stone corridor was not very long and as soon as I left the area with the twisting vines, I could see the cliff. Neither Uncle Three nor Panzi was there; it looked as if they had gone back to look for a way out. I walked to the end of the stone corridor where the sacrificial platform was. Just as I was about to put Fats down and take a rest, I saw Uncle Three climbing out of an opening in the cliff not too far away.

I was afraid he might not see me so I waved and shouted, "Uncle Three, I'm here!"

He caught sight of me and almost broke into a smile, but then his expression changed and he pointed towards my back. I turned to see Fats sitting up. Behind him and out of his sight, the green-eyed fox-corpse sat watching me with his blank and heartless stare.

CHAPTER TWENTY-THREE

INNER AND OUTER COFFINS

It was impossible for me to turn away from that green gaze but although I was frozen in what was almost a trance, for some reason my thoughts were still very clear. The taste of copper in my mouth was very strong and I wondered if I had swallowed the piece from the belt after all. Perhaps somehow it was offering its protection.

When I heard the sounds of Uncle Three and the others rushing to my rescue, I knew immediately that this was a mistake. They had not yet felt the black magic that this fox-corpse could wield, and so had no idea of the danger we were in. If they blundered over to help, something terrible was bound to happen. I wanted to yell a warning to them, but it was as if something were stuck in my throat. Even with my mouth wide open, not a sound emerged.

But then I realized I could still move my hands. I made a gesture of two guns with my hands, each of them pointing at the head of the fox-corpse. My heart was screaming, Panzi, you have to be smart just this once. If you can't interpret this simple piece of body language, then you should just give up and eat shit for the rest of your life.

A gunshot crackled behind me and the head of the green-eyed fox-corpse exploded before my eyes. My mouth was still wide open from my failed warning attempt, and liquid from the corpse splashed right in my face.

I began to vomit; this stuff tasted worse than shit and I threw up everything but my intestines and stomach lining. I turned and saw Panzi clutching his wounds with one hand and making an OK gesture with the other. I cursed silently and wiped the fluid from the corpse off my face with my sleeve.

There was a fair amount of distance between where Uncle Three was and my position on the sacrificial platform. The terrain was covered with vines and could have been the death of him, but Uncle Three was quick and clever. He threw stones to distract the vines and then rushed safely past them.

Soon he climbed on top of the sacrificial platform. He was extremely worried about me and came quickly to be sure I was all right but as soon as he got within smelling range, he frowned and gagged. Annoyed by his fastidiousness, I ran to him and gave him a bear hug, which made him so nauseated that he almost passed out.

Since he and Big Kui were both safe, I needed to make them account for their abandonment of me and asked,

"Uncle Three, how could you guys have run away to leave me alone in that tomb? You scared the hell out of me! Why did you leave me by myself in such a dreadful place?"

In response, my uncle reached over and slapped Big Kui on the head. "I told this fucking guy not to touch anything but he wouldn't listen." Then he told me everything that had happened from the time that they disappeared.

They had found another opening in the wall of the ear chamber in that main tomb. In most cases where there is a wall opening in an ancient tomb, there's usually a secret room behind it. Naturally they didn't know that all the trapdoors hidden in this tomb opened downward, but Uncle Three was a sharp guy and discovered the ruse with a glance. Big Kui moved too quickly with too little thought, and before Uncle Three could stop him, he pressed the button of the trap. They fell down one flight into the Western Zhou dynasty tomb, just as we had earlier.

The plot got more and more involved from that point. Uncle Three made it sound so outrageous and confusing as he went on that I could make no sense of his story and soon begged him to stop telling me anything at all.

"You better believe me," Uncle Three said. "Take a look at what I found." He pulled a black box out of his bag—with a "kacha" noise, the box magically turned into a machine gun.

I had done some research on guns, and knew this gun was famous—it was a 9 mm Ayers folding machine gun with bullets the size of a cigarette, very light and easy to use.

Uncle Three said that while they were in the tunnel, they had found several bodies which had been carrying explosives, as well as this gun. The whole place was covered with bullet holes—it looked as though one hell of a battle had raged there.

I double-checked the gun and was puzzled. It looked as if that group of grave robbers had been equipped with sophisticated weapons, or at least much more so than we were. Who they could have been, these people who went in but did not come back out? Could they have all died in here? If not, where were they now?

As my thoughts ran on, I leaned back against the sacrificial platform. Who knew that this stone stage that appeared so solid couldn't bear my weight? Before my entire body had pressed against it, the platform suddenly sank halfway into the ground.

Thinking we had triggered a trap, all of us quickly ducked down. The next thing we knew a series of noises came from below our feet, ending with a loud crash near the end of the platform.

We went to take a look and found a huge hole in the gargantuan tree that stood behind the stone platform. From the hole there appeared a mammoth bronze coffin, fixed in place with chains which had been attached to the largest tree branch and then wrapped several times around the coffin.

Uncle Three was speechless and then with a sigh of relief said, "So here is the real coffin."

"Holy shit!" Big Kui cried. "A coffin this big must be really valuable. Our trip hasn't been completely in vain!"

Uncle Three slapped him on his head and said, "Valuable?! Stop thinking about goddamn money all the time. Even if this thing was worth something, you still wouldn't be able to move it out of here. There's one inner coffin and one outer coffin involved here—not a simple casket. Damn you, don't always make me lose face with your greed and stupidity."

Big Kui scratched his head and dared not speak again. I looked closely, feeling something was wrong, and remarked to Uncle Three, "This is strange. Coffins of common people usually are nailed shut because nobody expects them to be opened again—but look. The traps placed in the platform seemed to have been put there to help us locate this. Could it be that the occupier of this grave wanted someone to open his coffin? Plus, you see here, these tightly wrapped chains don't seem intended to keep the coffin in place but to keep whatever was inside it from getting out."

Uncle Three nodded and we looked at each other questioningly. Could another monster be inside this coffin? Should we open it or leave it alone?

Uncle Three spat and decided, "My guess is everything that's valuable must be here in this coffin.

23. INNER AND OUTER COFFINS

If we leave now, then wouldn't our trip be pointless? So what if there's a monster in there? We have guns and explosives. If there's something in there, we'll fight the fucking thing!"

I nodded, and Uncle Three continued, "Besides, it's not likely now that we'll be able to get out the same way we came in. Nearly all of the cave openings on these cliffs will lead us to the tunnel maze again. To leave from one of them will take us forever. Our best hope is to climb from here."

We raised our heads and saw the crevice on the cavern's ceiling where moonbeams streamed through; what they revealed looked bleak and dreary. Uncle Three pointed to the giant tree. "You see, the top of this tree is very close to the ceiling. It has many branches, which should make it easy for us to climb it. Look at all of these vines that have grown as high as the top of this cave—they make a natural ladder."

"Master Three, what nonsense is this? This is a man-eating tree," Panzi argued. "Isn't climbing it the same thing as committing suicide?"

Uncle Three laughed. "This is a hydra-cypress. I've already thought this through earlier. Don't you see how the vines won't grow on the stones here? That's because this is Tianxin rock, which repels the hydra-cypress and its vines. If we coat ourselves with the dust from these stones, I guarantee we will climb unharmed and everything will proceed smoothly without a hitch."

"Will it really work?" Big Kui whimpered.

Uncle Three stared at him and I was sure he was going to slap Big Kui on the head one more time but instead he muttered, "Okay, shit—let's put some on and find out!"

Without another word, we scurried into action. With Fats on Big Kui's back and Uncle Three supporting Panzi, I shouldered our equipment and took a look back at the cave, thinking, We're all safe, but what about Poker-face? Uncle Three knew what was on my mind and assured me, "Menyouping can take care of himself—don't you worry."

I nodded, realizing I was the last man on earth to worry about Poker-face. He was much savvier than I was, and he seemed to possess supernatural powers. If there was any need for concern on anyone's behalf, he should be worrying about me.

Holding a gun, I led the way as we slowly reached the stone platform. A moment ago as we ran down the steps, we didn't notice that the entire platform was supported by huge boulders of Tianxin rock, so enormous that I couldn't figure out how they were brought in from outside.

Finally we reached the hole in the tree, and the giant bronze coffin stood before us. It was at least two and a half meters long, with ancient inscriptions engraved all over it.

We were all dead silent as if we were reluctant to disturb the occupant of this coffin. Uncle Three took out a crowbar and knocked on the surface, producing a flat, dull thud from inside, which made us realize it was absolutely crammed with objects. Uncle Three knew I had some knowledge of ancient inscriptions and asked me, "Can you read what's written on here?"

I shook my head and replied, "I don't understand the specifics, but I am sure the owner of the tomb is the one we have been looking for. The script on this coffin probably provides an outline of his life. It looks like he died before turning fifty without having fathered any children. The scenario in which he passed away is the same as I had read earlier. He died sitting like a Buddhist monk before the Emperor of the State of Lu. All the other texts are probably about his general life."

Uninterested in the personages and culture of the State of Lu, I scanned the inscriptions quickly.

"What do those words mean?" Big Kui asked. I took a look and saw the word *Open* in the middle of the coffin. Then there were other words that were bigger and more eye-catching than the others, which I knew indicated a date. "This should mark the date that the coffin was placed here, but I can't read the words so don't know what date it is," I explained.

While I examined the inscriptions, Uncle Three looked for the best way to open the coffin. He shook the chains and found they were all as thick as his thumb. After so many years of wear and tear, most of them were no longer in good shape and basically served only a decorative purpose.

Motioning to me to step back, my uncle scolded, "Stop wasting time with those inscriptions. Check them out after we open the coffin."

He had barely finished his sentence when the coffin began to shake, with a muffled noise coming from inside. At first I thought I was imagining things, and was about to ask the others if they heard something as well. Then suddenly there was still more quaking; I heard the noise again and knew it was real this time. My heart stopped for a second and I thought, Shit! Something terrible is trying to get out of there.

CHAPTER TWENTY-FOUR

RELEASING THE ZOMBIE

Panic-stricken, we all took a few steps backward. The quaking of the coffin meant that its occupant could move—and any sort of motion inside a coffin was not a good sign.

Big Kui turned pale. Trembling, he said, "It looks like there's something alive in here. Master Three, I think we should leave this coffin alone."

Uncle Three took a closer look at the seams of the coffin, shook his head, and said, "It's impossible. This coffin is very well sealed with no air flow. No matter if a living thing was put in there, it would have suffocated long ago. To make it even less possible, there's an exterior coffin and then an inner one, with probably several more layers inside. Let's pry into it a little and listen carefully."

I tried to estimate the approximate weight of the coffin. According to my memory, the heaviest bronze coffin ever found was a set of gigantic drum-roll coffins belonging to a noble named Zeng, which had weighed about nine tons. The shape of the coffin before us looked similar, but while the coffins in the

Zeng tomb were made of both bronze and wood, our discovery was made completely of bronze. So although I assumed that this coffin weighed far more than nine tons, I could not determine the precise weight.

Big Kui and Uncle Three first used their knives to scratch off the wax that sealed the seams. Then they slid in their crowbars and, with a grunt, pressed downward with all their might. We heard a bang and saw that their efforts had crumpled the bronze coffin lid. I darted over to help open the lid, which felt as though it weighed a ton. It took a long time until half of it had been moved and by then we were all out of breath and near exhaustion. Finally, as we all pushed, the lid opened and the inner part of the coffin was exposed.

It was an exquisite jade covering coated with lacquer, with jade stones around its edges. Nestled inside this jade wrapping was a wooden coffin, its surface covered with paintings.

Panzi's eyes almost fell out of his head when he saw the jade covering. As he clutched his wounded belly, his face was a mixture of joyful greed and physical pain. "Fuck," he yelped, "my share of this jade will let me do whatever I want for the rest of my life!"

"Absurd! This is jade from Manasi in Xinjiang," Uncle Three barked at him. "If you break it up into bits and sell the pieces, you will only get about a few hundred thousand dollars, which when shared with all of us isn't worth our time. We have to bring this out intact and undamaged for it to be worth anything."

Since he'd already caused enough trouble for everyone, Panzi calmed down after one look from Uncle Three. Scratching his head, he stepped away from the jade that tempted him so much.

Tapping the wooden coffin, Uncle Three observed, "Normally, the noblemen of the Warring States Period were buried with two outer coffins and three inner ones. If the tree was to be counted as the first outer coffin, then the bronze one is the second. This wooden coffin should be the most precious." With his knife, he carefully removed a number of gold threads that attached the jade wrapper to the painted coffin, doing this with painstaking caution so as not to ruin the protective cover. After half an hour, he was finally able to remove the outer jade covering to reveal what it had protected.

Uncle Three delicately folded the jade coffin cover and put it in his backpack. I picked it up and found it was deadweight and would be a tough load to carry.

Once the cover was removed, I could see the paintings on the wooden coffin, which were easier to decode than the inscriptions. I turned on my lamp and looked closely.

Painted on the coffin were a few drawings. The drawing on the coffin lid showed the scene when the body was first put in the coffin and placed down in the tomb. I saw a huge tree with a crack in the middle. The bronze coffin, uncovered, was carried by skeletons, with many people respectfully kneeling as it passed them.

24. RELEASING THE ZOMBIE

Encouraged by our findings, Big Kui's spirits were high, and he began to tug at the wooden coffin. Uncle Three pulled him back and yelled, "Every time you think you see a ghost you faint. Now that you see money, you're more than willing to risk your life. There is another layer below this, so don't screw this up. Move slowly and carefully." Then he squatted down and pressed his ear against the coffin as he gestured for us to be quiet.

We all held our breath while he listened for a long time. Then he turned around, ashen and trembling. "God damn it," my uncle said in a low voice, "it sounds like something's breathing in there."

By now, if we'd heard a ghost calling from inside the coffin, that would seem almost normal. But that something was living without oxygen inside a sealed box, breathing without air, was too incredible for us to comprehend. Big Kui was so frightened he could barely stammer, "It...it can't be a living corpse, can it?"

Uncle Three said, "Oh my ass! Don't give me any of your fucking bullshit now. We've come this far—do you want to tell me to put the lid back on the coffin?" Taking his black donkey hoof from where he kept it tucked in his shirt, he motioned toward me. I aimed my gun at the coffin while Big Kui picked up the crowbar, ready to bash the first thing that jumped out at us.

Uncle Three spat into his hands. He rolled his shoulders to relax his muscles and then inserted a crowbar into the coffin. As soon as he did this, a voice behind him cried, "Stop!"

We turned to see Fats, whom we thought was still unconscious. He waved his hand at us. "No, no. Something bad's going to happen if you open it like that. You guys with your little bit of half-assed experience, you think you can rob this grave? It's like turning on your flashlight in a latrine to look for shit. You don't know what you're doing."

"Then how would you open it?" Uncle Three looked ready to kill.

Fats waved his hand and motioned for Uncle Three to step away. Then he reached his hand into the cracks between the bronze coffin and the wooden one, closed his eyes, and fumbled around until his hand moved with a bullet's force. We heard a loud pop and as the lid of the coffin split lengthwise in half, we heard a cry of anguish coming from somewhere inside. I was so scared my muscles turned numb, and the gun almost fell out of my hand.

Fats jumped toward us and stretched his arms wide. He screamed, "Back!"

Without thinking, I aimed my gun at the coffin as I took several hasty steps backward. The painted wooden coffin rose up from the outer bronze one like a blooming lotus. The split lid that had covered it fell away on either side, revealing a sight within that took our breath away—a man dressed in black armor sitting bolt upright.

I raised my gun, ready to fire, but Fats grabbed my

24. RELEASING THE ZOMBIE

arm, saying, "Don't shoot—his armor is an incredible treasure. Don't destroy it!"

At last I could see what the legendary Ruler of Dead Soldiers looked like. He was what we call a moist corpse, a body that had not rotted away, but has retained all of its flesh, which is supple and resilient to the touch. His skin had become so white it almost looked translucent, like a very fine pearl, but his face was contorted as if he had died in agony and his eyes were tightly closed. It was surprising. If he had known how to preserve the female corpse so she still looked beautiful and peaceful in death, why did his own corpse not have that same appearance?

Uncle Three walked to the coffin's edge and said, "And I thought it was a goddamn zombie. Look here. There's a piece of wood propping him up from the back. No wonder he can sit up."

We all went to look and sure enough it was a trick. Once the coffin was opened, the corpse inside was pushed up by the wood that had been braced against his back to serve as a spring.

We all sighed with relief. I thought, this Ruler had prepared for every eventuality that might occur after his death. But he of all people should have known that men who were frightened by ghosts and spirits would not rob graves and that veteran grave robbers clung to no fears of that sort. While those inexperienced at this trade might have been shocked to death by his tricks, that we dared to open his coffin in the dead of night proved our fearlessness. These picayune scare tactics that he had devised were rather demeaning to men like us.

We drew closer to the corpse and decided the armor that he was wearing served as the third inner coffin. I identified it as Gold-thread Jade Armor, but I couldn't explain why the jade had turned black.

I came closer to the body and gasped. The corpse's chest was rising up and down as though he was breathing and I could distinctly hear the sounds of respiration. I was almost certain I could see a cloud of moisture coming from his nostrils.

Big Kui's jaw dropped as he squealed, "This…this… this goddamn thing seems to be alive!"

CHAPTER TWENTY-FIVE

THE JADE BURIAL ARMOR

"How can this corpse possibly be breathing?" I asked. "Have you ever seen anything like this before?"

"Of course not," Big Kui mumbled. "If I had to go through this sort of bullshit often, I'd be cleaning toilets instead of robbing graves."

I glanced over at Panzi, who was still clutching his wounded belly and sweating heavily. "Never mind what it is," he growled, "just fire an ammunition clip at it. If it's not dead now, it will be then. If you wait any longer, we'll all be in trouble once he stands up."

This was a sensible argument, I decided—better to take action without thinking than to think after you're dead and buried. Do something and do it fast.

As I aimed, Uncle Three and Fats anxiously waved their hands and cried out at the same time, "Wait...wait, wait!"

As he said this, Uncle Three was already beside the corpse. He waved his hands at me again and gaped as he studied the armor. Pointing at it, he gasped, "This...isn't this jade burial armor? My God—this really exists!"

Not knowing why he was so excited, I looked at my

uncle apprehensively. He was so worked up that he was close to tears as he stuttered, "Holy...Holy Mother of God! I have been robbing graves for so long, and finally...finally I found a real honest-to-God treasure. It's truly jade burial armor." He grabbed my shoulders. "He will stay alive and rejuvenated and continue to grow young as long as he is completely enveloped by this armor. It's not just something from a story. This corpse proves it's real."

In the era when this corpse walked the earth as a living man, one was considered old if he lived to be forty to fifty. Although the muscles of this corpse were a bit shrunken, the man's face indeed looked very young. It was amazing and I wondered, could there really be rejuvenation in this world?

Fats couldn't take his eyes off the armor. "I can't believe it," he said. "Not even the first Chinese emperor was able to find this armor. And it was on this guy all along. Master Three—there you are—do you know how to remove this thing from the body?"

Uncle Three shook his head. "I've heard that you can't take it off from the outside. Here's our problem—can we carry away the corpse while it is still wearing this?"

Both of them strolled back and forth as they analyzed the situation. They pulled the corpse's arms and legs occasionally, but it showed no signs of ill temper, nor did it seem dangerous. My heart resumed its normal pulse rate as I asked, "What would happen to the corpse inside if the armor were removed from the body?"

"Well, that I don't really know," Fats answered. "At the

worst he'll completely vanish into thin air."

I said, "He was doing fine before we came along. If we do that, aren't we committing murder?"

Fats almost fell down from laughter. "Young comrade, if every grave robber had your ideals and fine conscience, then we would never achieve anything. How few of these ancient nobles did not have bloodstained hands? Even if he were taken out alive and intact, he still ought to be executed for all the evil he did in his life. To worry the way you are is to ask for trouble."

He was right. It was wrong for me to stand idle, thinking and worrying while the others were so busy working. I went over to check what was in the coffin and found on the bottom a thick layer of something that looked like scales. I picked up a handful and asked, "What's this?"

Uncle Three sniffed it and replied, "That's the skin that came off his body."

Feeling my stomach somersault, I dropped the scales immediately, cursing. "Holy shit. Did this guy have a disease that caused so much of his skin to fall off?"

"Don't talk rubbish," my uncle snapped at me. "This is the old skin that fell from his body as he rejuvenated. Every time a layer fell off, he became younger. He probably lost five or six layers, judging by this amount of skin."

I looked again. It looked absolutely disgusting, like snake skin, not human flesh. Just before I puked, Fats yelled, "There's something over here!"

We rushed to look but all we could see was a tiny bit

of thread hanging under the armpit of the burial figure. "Fats, your vision is too sharp for its own good. Not even a piece of fucking lint can escape your exacting attention," I sneered.

Fats stared at me and whispered, "You southern comrades are savages who always destroy burial sites as you plunder them. Grave robbing is a meticulous art— don't you know this yet? If you didn't have me along, you guys would already have obliterated the corpse in order to remove this armor."

Uncle Three, feeling as though he was losing face, said, "Fuck you. We don't even know if you're telling the truth. My nephew may be right—this may just be a piece of useless lint."

Fats laughed. "And you still don't believe me." As he began to pull on the thread, we heard a sharp noise. Something flashed before my eyes like a flare of lightning.

Uncle Three's reaction was almost that fast. He dropped Fats with a kick on the butt as a knife whizzed into a tree trunk with a velocity that buried it deep in the wood. If not for Uncle Three's kick, that knife would have pierced right through Fats's skull.

We jumped back and saw Poker-face standing near the steps of the platform. His body was soaked with blood and his clothing was torn almost to ribbons. Plainly visible was a tattoo that his clothes had previously concealed—an image of a green unicorn, the legendary *qilin*, so large that it looked as though it covered the entire back of his body. His left hand was still poised in a knife-throwing position and the other held a strange object. When we looked closely, we all gasped—it was the severed head of a blood zombie.

He barely glanced at us as he limped up the stairs onto the platform, breathing heavily. Judging by his deep gashes and bruises, he had been in a hard-fought battle. He took a look at the coffin, and said very quietly, "Get out of the way."

The veins on Fats's forehead were about to explode and I really couldn't blame him for being enraged. He jumped up and screamed, "What the fuck did you just do that for?"

Poker-face turned his head and stared at him coldly, "To kill you."

Fats rolled up his sleeves and stormed over toward Poker-face but Big Kui stopped him. Uncle Three could tell this situation could scuttle our expedition and tried to smooth things over. "Don't panic. Menyouping certainly must have a reason for what he just did. Let's hear him out—and don't forget—he's already has saved your life once or twice on this journey, right? Calm down."

Fats stopped struggling for a few seconds and then agreed with my uncle. He freed himself from Big Kui's grasp and angrily plopped down on the ground, muttering, "You fuckers are sticking together and I can hardly fight all of you by myself. I give up—whatever you say."

Poker-face put his bloody trophy on the jade bed. He coughed and said, "This blood zombie is the true owner

of the jade burial armor. The Ruler of Dead Soldiers
stole it and the original owner turned into this monster
as a result. When someone puts on this armor he will
shed his skin once every five hundred years. He can
safely remove it only during the time his skin is peeling;
otherwise he instantly will turn into a blood zombie
the minute he takes off the jade armor. The corpse that
you see in the coffin before you has already lived three
thousand years. If you had pulled that thread a moment
ago, he would have awakened and then we would all be
corpses in this place."

He coughed a few more times after he finished and
blood came out of the corner of his mouth. He was badly
hurt from some internal injury, that was plain to see.

Panzi, who was still in a lot of pain, stood in a corner
without saying a word, but suddenly he burst out,
"Listen, I'm a straightforward bastard, so please don't
be pissed off at what I have to say to you. You know way
too much—more than any of the rest of us. If you don't
mind, please explain how this is possible; there's no harm
in that. I don't know what kind of god on earth you may
be but I know you saved my life. If I get out of here in
one piece, I will certainly come to wherever you live and
thank you in a way that you deserve."

Panzi's words were quite articulate and respectful; I
figured Poker-face would be unable to resist them. But he
kept silent as if he had heard nothing. He walked to the
Ruler's corpse and looked him up and down. Suddenly
his eyes gleamed with hatred and before anyone realized
what he was doing, his hand was already on the corpse's

neck in a stranglehold.

A shriek came from the corpse's throat, and his body began to shake violently. Coldly Poker-face looked the dead man in the eye, saying, "You've lived long enough. Now die—hell has been waiting for you to arrive."

As he applied more pressure, the veins protruded on his arms, and soon a bone-cracking noise echoed all around us. The corpse moaned; his legs shivered and kicked one last time, and then his skin turned completely black.

Stunned and speechless, we all stared at Poker-face as he tossed the corpse aside as if it was just worthless garbage. I grabbed his arm, shouting, "Who the hell are you and why do you hate this corpse?"

He looked at me for a few seconds before saying, "What the fuck is it to you?"

"What have you done? We fought our way down to this grave with every scrap of strength we have," Fats yelled. "It was tough enough just to get this damn coffin open. Then you waltz in without saying a fucking word and strangle this living zombie to death. You at least owe us a goddamn explanation!"

Poker-face turned his head and looked at the bloody skull that he had placed on the jade bed. Somber and despondent, he pointed to a small purple jade box that was in the painted wood coffin and said, "You'll find everything you want to know inside that box."

CHAPTER TWENTY-SIX
SECRET OF THE PURPLE JADE BOX

Purple jade is the same stone as serpentine. It is generally used to make an amulet or an object to exorcise evil spirits—not to craft a little box. It was especially unusual that the box seemed to have been carved from a single block of serpentine and then trimmed with gold.

Since it had been placed where the corpse's head had been, it seemed to have been used as its pillow. Pillows made of ordinary jade are immensely rare; one made from serpentine was even more valuable—it was priceless. It was quite probable that not even emperors at that time had been honored in this fashion.

We placed the box on the ground with extreme caution. There was no lock and we opened it carefully. Within it was a scroll of yellow silk brocade with gold trimming. The gold was woven into the fabric and was beautifully preserved. Unfolding the scroll, we saw written on the top left corner: *The Book of the Ruler of Dead Soldiers*.

Fats was completely uninterested in the scroll since he couldn't understand the writing on it. He muttered to himself and went over to examine the jade armor. Poker-face pulled out the knife he had hurled into the tree and lay down on one side of the jade bed. He silently stared at the corpse he had strangled, and his eyes became blurred.

Uncle Three and I sat beside him and carefully pored over the text on the silk scroll. I could only read fragments of paragraphs but when I linked the fragments together, I could figure out the gist of the text.

The records detailed in this Book of the Ruler of Dead Soldiers were simply outrageous and unthinkable. If I had not experienced so many strange occurrences already, I would never have believed such things could happen in this world.

On the edge of the scroll was a small paragraph of text that the Ruler had written himself. It was only a few lines, recounting all the important events that happened from his birth to his death. To translate all of this would take me at least half a month or more, but I could immediately understand the two most important things it said.

First came a concise account of how the Ruler obtained the devil's imperial seal, which I deciphered and then read aloud to my companions.

He had inherited his father's official status when he was twenty-five years old. He worked on the tomb excavation team for the State of Lu and paid his soldiers with the gold he found in the tombs.

One day he entered a tomb where he found a serpent lying beside the coffin.

The Ruler was very brave. He reasoned that there must

be some evildoer inside the reptile so he chopped it in half with his sword. He issued an order for the snake to be disemboweled, and within its body was found a box made out of purple-enameled gold.

As I read this, my heart pounded. Could the box in my bag be the same one that was discovered inside the serpent? I paused but my uncle looked at me impatiently and said, "Don't stop. Go on!" I put my thoughts aside for the time being and continued to read aloud.

The Ruler didn't think the box was important, only an object the serpent had found and swallowed. But later when he slept, he dreamed of a white-bearded old man who asked, "Why did you kill me?"

The Ruler of Dead Soldiers was a violent man. He killed often and then forgot about it. He had no idea who this old man was, and answered, " I kill whenever I choose and whomever I choose."

The old man suddenly turned into a serpent and started to attack him, but the Ruler was as fierce in his dreams as he was in the battlefield. Taking his sword, he stabbed the serpent, kicked it several times, and was preparing to behead it, but the serpent begged for mercy, pointing out that, since its flesh had already been destroyed, it would never be able to achieve resurrection if its spirit was also killed.

Bargaining with the Ruler, it promised that if he would let it go, two treasures would be given to him, and a government ministry as well. Although he was answerable only to the emperor, as a soldier and grave robber his status was low, so the Ruler of Dead Soldiers agreed to spare the life of the snake's spirit.

The serpent told him how to open the purple-enameled gold box that had been found in its belly and how to use the treasures that were kept inside. After the Ruler had finished listening to the snake and knew all of its secrets, he picked up his sword and cut off its head.

Fats ran over to me when he heard me read this and asked, "One of the treasures must be the devil's imperial seal. What was the other one? There was no record in the ancient books. Could it be this jade burial armor?"

I gestured for him to shut up and went on with my reading.

After the Ruler of Dead Soldiers woke up the next morning, he did as the snake had told him in his dream and opened the box easily. But nothing I read told us what treasures he found within it, only that after he had used them once "quite smoothly," he felt that this must be kept an airtight secret. So he killed all the members of his entourage and everyone in their families—even a baby who was less than a month old.

As I read this, I felt sick—how could anyone be so vicious and merciless?

Fats asked, "How could one man kill so many people? He must have used what was in the box to be able to accomplish that sort of feat. Shit, I'm going to die if you don't read faster and find out what the two treasures were."

"What the hell are you chattering about like an old woman?" I yelled at him. "Just go play with your burial armor and stop bothering me."

He grinned. "Calm down, it's okay, I have to interrupt. I'm so keyed up, my guts are itching—read faster, damn your eyes!"

I ignored him and continued.

Because of his two treasures, the Ruler of Dead Soldiers was invincible for the next few decades in both war and affairs of the state, and his reputation soared. But in his later years, due to frequent contact with dead bodies, he fell ill and his own body grew weak. In the end, the emperor stripped him of his military power when he became old and feeble. He was only responsible for robbing graves and was no longer used in battle, which of course meant that he had been demoted.

As his health declined more and more each day, he began to feel afraid of death. One day, he dreamed of the serpent he had killed several decades before, who now told him that it was his turn to die and that everyone was waiting for him in the world of the dead. When the Ruler looked around, he was horrified to see that waiting for him were all the people he had viciously and mercilessly killed during his lifetime.

When he awoke and recalled the details of the dream, he was terror-stricken and went to ask for advice from his military counselor.

This was a man named Mr. Iron-face, a master of numerology and Feng Shui. He gave the issue some thought, and said that there was a suit of jade armor that when put on, rejuvenated its wearer to be as he was when still a youth and made him immortal as well. However, it had vanished long ago, and to find it one would have to go into the ancient tombs.

These words gave the Ruler a glimmer of hope in the midst of his fear and despair—after all, grave robbing was his specialty and he did this better than anyone else alive. All that night he read every ancient book that he could find, which in that period contained knowledge that is now lost to us. Finally, in one of the books he learned that the jade armor was to be found in a large tomb.

Mobilizing three thousand men, he spent more than half a year excavating a cave in a mountain, where he discovered an immense imperial tomb of the Western Zhou dynasty.

It had been built by burrowing into a mountain and then using the natural caves found inside. The interior tunnels were constructed by the principle of the Eight Diagrams and were extremely complex. The strangest thing inside the cave where the main tomb was located was a gigantic tree, which the Ruler named hydra-cypress. A young male corpse sat under it in a meditative position, wearing a suit of black jade burial armor.

Mr. Iron-face had a look and decided that this was indeed the jade armor they had been looking for. The young male corpse who wore it looked half-alive and half-dead. Every so often, the dead skin on his body peeled away and beneath it was a new layer of skin. Mr. Iron-face believed when this young man died, he was doubtless a withered old man.

Mr. Iron-face was a competent, intelligent man who knew how to prevent blood zombies from becoming powerful, and he used a special method to remove the male corpse from the armor. Then he sealed the corpse inside a stone coffin and placed it in a nearby tomb of secondary importance.

Following the plan constructed for him by Mr. Iron-face, the Ruler of Dead Soldiers swallowed a harmless pill that he told everyone was deadly poison and pretended to die before the eyes of the emperor. Believing the Ruler could really come and go freely between the human world and the world of the dead and fearing his power, the emperor gave him a funeral much grander than those of any of the other noblemen in the State of Lu.

The Ruler of Dead Soldiers, while excavating the cave, had built a fanlike tomb on top of the Western Zhou imperial tomb. Because he was an expert grave robber, he set many cunning traps to mislead anyone who might come to the cave, including the trap of the Seven Deceptive Coffins, then hid himself in the tomb of the Western Zhou dynasty which he placed inside the thousand-year-old hydra-cypress.

Before he entered his own coffin, he killed every worker who was involved in this project by drowning them in the river. Then he poisoned the rest of his entourage, leaving only a man and a woman who were his two most loyal subordinates to place him inside the coffin. After these two people had completed their tasks, they committed suicide by taking poison.

By the time I finished reading I was convinced that most of the ancient corpses in the carcass cave we had found at the beginning of our journey had probably been killed by the Ruler.

"It doesn't say what happened to Mr. Iron-face," I asked my uncle, "Could he have been interred with the dead?"

Uncle Three shook his head and said, "That type of person is very clever. He must have known beforehand that the Ruler would kill everyone to prevent his secrets from being divulged. He would not so blindly let himself be buried with the murdered bodies."

"Of course not," Poker-face muttered. "Because the person lying in that jade armor is not the Ruler of Dead Soldiers—it's Mr. Iron-face."

CHAPTER TWENTY-SEVEN
A LIE

Once I heard this, a flash of light crossed through my mind as if I had come up with the solution myself. "So the two were switched at the last minute?" I asked.

Poker-face nodded. He looked at the corpse and said, "This person was incessantly scheming all along. He only wanted to use the influence of the Ruler of Dead Soldiers in order to achieve his own goal of immortality."

"How do you know all this? You seem like you've lived through it all yourself."

"Of course I didn't live through it," Poker-face shook his head. "A few years ago I went to rob a grave from the Song dynasty and found a complete silk manuscript from the Warring States Period. It was Mr. Iron-face's autobiography. After he gave the Ruler all of the details of his plan, he set his own home on fire and burned his entire family to death. He threw in the body of a beggar so people would believe he had died in the fire as well, and then disguised himself as a beggar in order to escape detection. Finally, he waited for the Ruler of Dead Soldiers to be buried, and then easily sneaked into the tomb. He dragged the frail and powerless Ruler out of the jade armor and put it on himself. With all of the trouble the Ruler of Dead Soldiers had gone through, he ended up at last as somebody else's pawn."

Shocked and bewildered, I said, "When the Ruler's corpse was dragged out of the armor, doesn't that mean that created another blood zombie? So aren't there two somewhere in this place?"

"Mr. Iron-face didn't say anything about that in his autobiography. Perhaps the time that the Ruler spent within the jade armor was too short for him to have become a blood zombie." Poker-face's eyes looked a little uneasy as he embarked upon this theory. "Mr. Iron-face probably didn't enlarge upon this in his autobiography because it was never an issue."

I glanced at Poker-face and for some reason I felt he wasn't telling us everything he knew. I looked over at Uncle Three and saw that he also looked doubtful. But after Poker-face finished speaking, he acted as if there was no more to be said. Recovering his usual emotionless countenance, he stood up and said, "It's almost daybreak. We had better be going."

"No way. We haven't found the devil's imperial seal yet!" Fats yelped. "You can see all the good stuff that's in here—wouldn't we be fools if we left without the treasures we've been seeking all along?"

Poker-face stared at him coldly and with a certain measure of hostility in his gaze. Fats shrugged and muttered, "All right, all right. But we have to get this jade armor out somehow, right? It's probably the only one of its kind on this entire planet. I'm only looking out for all of our interests here."

That seemed to make sense. Uncle Three slapped Fats on the butt and said, "Then why are you dawdling around in slow motion? Do what you have to do and let's get out of this fucking place!"

Suddenly I lost all interest in what they were about to do, and did not want to help. I closed my eyes to take a break and felt a few drops of water fall on my face.

I thought it had begun to rain, opened my eyes to look, and there was the blood zombie's severed head, peering over the side of the jade bed. His eerie eyes were fixed upon my own eyebrows.

Leaping up in fear, I saw the head roll off the bed and fall to the ground; it looked to me as if there was something hidden inside its skull. Fats moved to look more closely but he was pulled back by Poker-face who warned, "Don't move. Let's observe this."

As Fats nodded, we all saw a tiny red corpse-eating bug chew its way through the zombie's scalp and climb out. Big Kui saw it and screamed, "Shit! How dare this tiny fucker show his face anywhere near me?" He raised his crowbar, ready to crush the insect.

Uncle Three held him back, saying, "You brainless moron. This is the goddamn king of all corpse-eaters—if you kill it, you'll be in big trouble."

Big Kui stared at my uncle in disbelief and asked, "This tiny thing is the king of corpse-eaters? How did the big ones let that happen?"

Poker-face looked shaken; he tapped my shoulder and said, "Let's get out of here now—if the king of the corpse-eating bugs is here, I won't be able to control any of those little bastards. They're extremely powerful when their leader is at hand."

The little red corpse-eater began to make its creaking sound, flapped its wings, looked in our direction, and came flying straight towards us. Poker-face screamed, "It's poisonous! You'll die if it touches you. Get out!"

Uncle Three came rapidly to our side but slow-witted Big Kui reached out and instinctively grabbed the bug with his right hand. He stood as still as a wooden statue for a second and then let out a hair-raising shriek. The flesh on his hand instantly turned bloodred and the color quickly spread up his arm to his shoulder.

"He's poisoned," Fats shouted. "Hurry up—cut off his arm!" He grabbed at Poker-face's sword, and taken by surprise, Poker-face let it fall. Catching it in midair, Fats sank to his knees, cursing, "Holy shit! How come this is so heavy?" He tried several times to pick up the sword but couldn't manage it.

It was too late. Big Kui was in such agony that his limbs began to twist convulsively. In only a few seconds, his entire body turned scarlet as if all of his skin was suddenly melting into lava.

He looked at his hand, opened his mouth to scream, and was unable to utter a noise. Poker-face saw that I wanted to go over and help, and pulled me back, saying sternly, "You can't touch him. Once you touch him, you'll die!"

Big Kui saw us backing away as if we were looking at a monster and became even more petrified. He rushed over to me with his mouth wide open as if shouting, "Help me!" I was too scared to move so Uncle Three dashed over and pulled me aside. Big Kui then jumped at the air like a madman and leaped towards Panzi. Panzi was in such bad shape that he couldn't react fast enough to save himself so Fats cried out and grabbed my gun. Knowing he was going to open fire, I began to fight with him to get it back and in the struggle, the gun went off.

We all heard the gunshot that struck Big Kui in the head. His body shook and he dropped to the ground.

A buzzing sounded in my head, and I fell to my knees. Everything was happening too fast. A minute ago I had been perfectly okay and now I was another person. My mind went blank and I had no idea of what to do.

The red corpse-eater made another creaking noise and, flapping its wings, crawled out of the palm of Big Kui's hand. Fats muttered to himself as Poker-face shouted, "Don't!" But it was too late. Fats had already run over, picked up the serpentine box and smashed the bug flat.

For a time not a sound could be heard in the cave. Then Poker-face abruptly picked up some stone dust from the ground and scattered it all over his body. He yelled, "Come on quick or it'll be too late!"

Fats looked around—nothing had happened. Surprised, he asked, "Why are we in such a rush?"

His voice had hardly faded when the dead silence in the cave was quickly filled with noise. Countless creaking sounds came from all directions. Then we saw from the openings on the cliffs, both large and small, one, two, three, ten, a hundred…an uncountable number of green corpse-eaters poured out. The scale of their empire could not be described by any words in any human language. They gushed out in wave after wave, ones in the rear crawling on top of the ones that led the way. They came in swarms, blotting out the sky and covering the earth.

I was stunned at the sight of them but Uncle Three smacked me on the head and shouted, "Run!"
He picked up Panzi and carried him on his back. Fats was still obsessed with the serpentine box and turned back to rescue it. Uncle Three yelled, "Aren't you worried about your goddamn life?" Seeing it was impossible to reach the box, Fats grabbed the gold-trimmed silk scroll instead and stuffed it in his pocket.

We all scrambled up the tree, grateful for the many concave and convex spots on the leafy branches, making it an easy climb. At the same time, all the corpse-eaters had surged toward the bottom of the tree—I looked down and saw the entire base of the hydra-cypress was covered with a green swarm. If anyone of us fell, not even a splinter of his bones would be left.

The corpse-eaters gathered together, and suddenly began to leap upward. They were much faster at climbing trees than we were and they were soon at our ankles.

Fats, climbing in front of me, turned and asked, "Didn't you say that weird guy's blood was more powerful than mosquito repellent against these creatures? Why don't we spill a little of it to use now?"

My mind was still reliving the scene of Big Kui falling down dead just a moment ago. I simply didn't care about anything Fats had to say. He saw I had no intention of discussing his suggestion and muttered, "Fuck your

27. A LIE

mother." Suddenly I felt a sharp pain on my leg—a corpse-eater had bitten me on my calf. I kicked it off and looked down again at what resembled a pot boiling with corpse-eaters, all scrambling their way up the tree.

Uncle Three yelled from above me, "Explosives! There's a bag of explosives on the side of the jade bed!"

I asked, "Where?"

Uncle Three cursed, "You were sitting by the goddamn edge of the bed and you don't remember seeing it—it's on the left side." I looked down and could only see an ocean of corpse-eaters. Their bodies had already buried the jade bed and the bag of explosives. Firing a few gunshots, I hit perhaps only a dozen among thousands of the bugs. Then I saw Poker-face take a bunch of matches from his pocket, light them and throw them down at the spot where we knew the bed was.

Although the corpse-eaters were no longer deterred by Poker-face's blood, they were still terrified of fire. Once the flaming matches hit the ground, the insects quickly retreated and formed a huge open circle, leaving the backpack with its load of explosives exposed to view.

A few bugs clung to Fats's butt and he screamed, "God damn it! Light those firecrackers quickly. I can't hold on any longer!"

Panzi shouted from above, "Shit! No way. There's too much firepower in that bag—blow it up and we're all going to hell!"

More and more corpse-eaters had crawled up the tree and I knew that to hesitate now meant a slow and agonizing death for all of us. I screamed, "Who cares at this point? If we die, let's die quickly!" Gritting my teeth, I fired at the bag.

The explosion went off immediately. I heard a loud crash, wobbled a bit, and felt like my chin, butt, and thighs were all hit by a pile driver at the same time. My whole body soared from the force of the blast, then I collided heavily with God-knows-what. My head was whirling and reeling. My throat turned wet, and I spat out blood. Everything before my eyes went black, there was a faint ringing in my head, and I couldn't hear a thing.

It was a while before I could prop myself up. I looked and saw that many corpse-eaters below us had been blasted into smithereens, I looked for my companions but saw nobody. Hurriedly, I moved my arms and legs to continue my ascent.

Because I had coated myself with a layer of the dust from the stone platform, the devil-armed vines moved away from me in droves, but there was a new wave of sound below. I looked down to see the corpse-eaters again surging forward. They were crawling rapidly and I knew I had to keep going no matter how much pain I was in. Closing my eyes, I climbed upward like a crazed baboon.

I was almost up to the crevice in the roof of the cavern when I felt a twinge on my back. I turned my head and saw a corpse-eater had jumped upon me and was biting viciously. I shot it dead just as an even bigger one attacked my thigh. Gritting my teeth against the pain, I shot it, but by then a third and a fourth had already jumped on my body.

I was only a few feet away from the crack in the roof

which gave me a new surge of energy and strength. I thought, Go ahead and bite—you only have a little more time, which is not as much as you need to kill me. You're all going to die once I get out of this hellhole.

As I climbed, I suddenly felt another presence, looked, and saw a bloody face peering out from behind the tree trunk. His eyeballs were staring straight at me, looking as if they were about to burst out of their sockets.

CHAPTER TWENTY-EIGHT
FIRE

The face was badly mutilated. I couldn't see if the
skin had melted and exposed the muscles inside, or if
blood was oozing from its body to cover its face. All of
a sudden I realized this was someone I knew—looking
carefully, I recognized Big Kui.

A bullet had trimmed away a layer of skin on the left
side of his head, exposing the bones of his skull. But it
had not seemed to have gone into his brain and I felt
some hope that even though even though his wounds
were serious, they didn't appear to be fatal.

"Big Kui, come with me," I called to him, "perhaps we
can save you."

He didn't move and his eyes stared at me resentfully,
as if he hated us for abandoning him. He grabbed my
hand and it took on the same hideous bloodred color
that covered his entire body. I felt a burst of burning
itchiness and I knew I was finished.

A faint voice came from Big Kui's mouth as he pulled
me downward. I thought of the horror of watching his
skin melting and with a burst of determination, I shook
away his hand. But then he grabbed my foot as if his

dying wish was for us to be together in hell.

I screamed, "Big Kui, let me go! Life is all anyone really wants—if you want to live, then climb up with me. Who knows? We may find a cure for what is killing you now."

My words only seemed to make him even more furious and he leaped upon me, his eyes radiating beams of evil. Grabbing me by the neck, he began to strangle me.

One of us was going to die, and it wasn't going to be me. I kicked him viciously and as his grip loosened, I aimed my gun at his chest and pulled the trigger. He hurtled away from me, his blood splashing in all directions. Both of his arms outstretched, he fell straight into the mass of corpse-eaters.

My hand that he had seized was so numb that I could feel nothing and I had no idea if it was still holding onto a branch or not. As my body slipped, I tried to grab onto one of the devil-armed vines with my other hand but since I was protected by rock dust, the vine drew away from me. I cursed in the dark as my body slid down, landing on a huge tree branch.

The branch was covered with corpse-eaters and some fell off when I landed. I gripped the branch with my legs to stop myself from sliding down any farther but found that the corpse-eaters were starting to surround me again.

I could not help but smile as I faced the bitter truth of my predicament. I had so many options of death to choose from—I could fall to death, have the bugs eat me to death, or be poisoned to death. With fate generously providing this bounty of choice in my hour of need, I should feel more gratitude than I was currently able to muster, I decided.

And then there was Fats, climbing up toward me, kicking a few corpse-eaters out of his way. He looked at me and yelled, "How the hell can you just lie here staring at me? See how many holes there are on my butt?"

When he came over to give me a hand, I shouted, "Don't touch me. I've been poisoned. Just go. You can't save me!"

Fats said nothing as he picked me up, laughing. "Find a mirror and take a good look at yourself. Your fucking complexion looks better than mine. In fact, your cheeks are as glowing and rosy as a pretty girl's. How could you be poisoned?"

Startled, I looked down and saw only a red rash on my hand that went up my arm, as if it had been bitten by thousands of mosquitoes. But it stopped at my shoulder and seemed to be slowly fading away. How could the poison have had no effect on me?

Fats hauled me on his back, gritted his teeth, and continued to climb as I served as his human shield—all the corpse-eaters now jumped on my butt and started biting me. I yelled, "You fat fuck! I thought you wanted to help me, but you just needed a goddamn shield!"

He shouted back, "What are you complaining about? If you're not satisfied, why don't you come and carry me? Don't you see I barely have any unbitten flesh left on my butt?"

I did not want to talk nonsense with him. There was a thick circle of corpses hanging close to the tree trunk of our hydra-cypress and occasionally Fats would bump into a pile of bones. Fortunately the corpse-eaters did the same thing, and they couldn't tell the difference between our living bodies and the corpses—many of them jumped on the corpses and started chomping away at the dead flesh that moved wildly as Fats collided with them.

Noticing this, Fats thought it worked to our advantage so he told me to push the bodies slightly and make them swing when I was able to touch them. Although it disgusted me, I did as he told me, hoping it might save our lives.

Every time I saw a corpse, I kicked it and soon the areas we went through were filled with spinning corpses. When it came to IQ levels, corpse-eaters were unfit to compete with humans. They had no idea whether it was better to chase after us or stop and feast on spinning corpses. Fats increased his speed, the distance between us and the corpse-eaters widened, and we finally felt it was safe to breathe a sigh of relief.

My arms and legs were no longer numb, and I began to think that the feeling I had when I was poisoned seemed to be the same thing my grandfather had documented in his journal when the blood zombie raced across his back. Grandfather survived. Could it be that, as one of his bloodline, I had inherited his immunity?

Now that my limbs were fully functional, Fats set me

28. FIRE

down. His face was sweaty, and he was panting like a dog in August. I remembered that when I had carried him on my back earlier, I had almost spat up blood. Now we were even.

Suddenly, behind Fats I saw someone on a branch waving at me. Trembling, I rubbed my eyes and the person disappeared. Thinking he had hidden behind the tree, I stuck my head out to investigate.

"Stop wasting time," Fats grumbled. "Come on."

"Wait a second!" I pulled him back. "Go left! I just saw someone waving."

We looked, and there was nothing but a hole in the tree that looked like the shape of a man. It was dark and I wondered what was inside.

Fats turned on his flashlight. There was a bunch of rolled-up vines in the hole wrapped around a rotting corpse of a man. His blue eyes were so clouded that it was impossible to make out where his pupils were, and his mouth was open as if he wanted to tell us something.

Fats sneered at me, "He's only a dead man. Maybe ghosts have begun to greet you with friendly waves, do you suppose?"

I had encountered too many strange things on this trip—whether ghosts were real or not wasn't something I wanted to debate with Fats. If this corpse had beckoned us over, he definitely had a reason, I thought. As I stared at him, I saw he had something clutched in his hand. Prying his fingers open, I found a pendant in his death grip.

The corpse-eaters below were rattling again and had begun to climb up to us. I looked at the dead man, gave him a salute, and continued my climb. Fats and I both moved much faster than usual; we weren't too far from the crack in the cave's roof and reached it easily.

As we climbed through the opening, we looked down and saw that the corpse-eaters had no plans of stopping their assault. They had reached the edge of the crevice and Fats yelled, "It's not time to rest yet. Run!"

I had been underground for so long that the openness of my new surroundings felt confusing to me. A man carrying something came running out of the bushes—it was Uncle Three. When he saw me, he shouted, "Quick—pour this gasoline everywhere!"

I ran to him and looked—where we had entered the tomb and the crevice we had just emerged from were separated only by a low cliff just several feet high. Our equipment was still there and when I saw the barrels of gasoline waiting for us, my heart soared and I thought, all right you little bastards—just wait and see what's in store for you now.

Fats and I leaped down, each grabbed a barrel, and ran back to my uncle. He was already pouring gas through the opening we had crawled through and down the walls of the cave. As the corpse-eaters approached the crevice, Uncle Three lit a cluster of matches and tossed the flaming bundle into the crack in the roof.

A fireball shot into the air and the smell of hellfire filled our nostrils. The tide of corpse-eaters retreated in a flash as the gasoline formed a wall of fire. We heard

28. FIRE

them wailing in agony as they burned alive, and it sounded wonderful.

Adding more fuel to the conflagration by pouring in our remaining barrels of gas, we watched the fire erupt from the crevice to a height taller than two men put together.

We were struck by a wave of intense heat that singed off my eyebrows, and, taking a few steps back, I looked at the pendant that I held tightly in my hand. It was a name tag for James—perhaps the corpse I took it from? I polished it on my sleeve and put it in my pocket, thinking if I had the chance, I would find his family and give this to them so he might rest in peace.

Fats was sweating like fifty pigs from the heat of our inferno. He asked Uncle Three, "Where are the other two?"

Uncle Three pointed behind us. "Panzi's out of it. It looks like he's got a fever. As for Menyouping, I haven't seen him anywhere. I thought he was with you guys."

I glanced at Fats and he sighed, "I haven't seen him—I'll bet he didn't make it."

Uncle Three shook his head and said, "No. This guy comes and goes mysteriously—and he was ahead of all of us the whole time. If he had been caught in the explosion, he would probably have been blasted out of the cave and we would have seen him."

I looked at Uncle Three's expression and knew that he really wasn't very confident about Poker-face's safety. Although it was true he was an expert grave robber, he'd been in the same mess as we were before the explosives went off. If he had been flung out of the tree by the blast, he was dead for sure.

We looked around within the vicinity but without success. There was no sign of Poker-face.

We returned to the camp, packed our things, and lit a bonfire to heat the canned food that we'd packed in our bags. I was unbearably hungry, and could have eaten anything put in front of me. As we ate, Uncle Three pointed at the low cliff behind us. "You see, this camp is right at the edge of the crevice. Obviously the tree demon that the old guy saw was the hydra-cypress. It was probably the noise from the celebration of the men he had guided that caused the tree to break through from the cave's roof. Good thing we didn't stay overnight here but went straight down into the tomb, or else we too would have been captured by the monstrous tree."

"We don't know how long our fire is going to last," Fats observed. "If it burns out, the corpse-eaters will come and we'll be in trouble. It's almost dawn. Let's hurry out of the forest and we'll talk about everything later."

I quickly took a few more bites of food and nodded. Fats and Uncle Three took turns carrying Panzi and we set off into the forest.

We were quiet as we traveled. When we first came to this place, we had talked and sung happily. Now we were completely focused on finding safety and jogged in silence. We knew we were fleeing for our lives.

My strength had reached its limit. In the last part of

28. FIRE

our walk, I was relying almost solely on willpower to carry me through. If a bed had appeared before me, I would have fallen asleep in less than two seconds—but none did.

We walked all that day and into the next morning before we got out of the forest. Passing the rocky slopes created by the landslide, we finally saw that sweet little village.

But we couldn't relax until we took Panzi to the village clinic. The country doctor came, frowned, and immediately called the nurses to come and help him. Sitting on a nearby stool, I fell asleep.

It was a sleep caused by severe exhaustion—deep, dark, and with no dreams. I only woke up because I heard a disturbance outside and wanted to know just what was going on.

CHAPTER TWENTY-NINE

THE PURPLE-ENAMELED GOLD BOX

I was a bit dazed and looked around for my uncle to see if he knew what was happening outside, but he was on the stool beside me, sleeping even more heavily than I had been. I ran outside and saw people pushing their carts and pulling their livestock up the hill behind the village. I heard a child yell as he ran past me, "Oh, no! Oh, no! There's a fire up on the mountain!"

I was shocked. Could the forest have been set ablaze by the conflagration we had started in the cavern? When we had lit a fire in the crevice of the cave, we hadn't thought of being careful and if there were a forest fire, we were no doubt the ones to be blamed.

I began to be upset—if this fire grew larger, it would do a lot of damage. What had we done? I ran inside to wake my uncle and we grabbed two chamber pots from under a hospital bed. Following the crowd, we ran up the hill. Fats came by on a big mule-drawn cart and shouted, "We caused a shitload of trouble here—come on! Let's go fight this fire!"

My uncle and I jumped on the cart and saw a huge cloud of black smoke in the distance. It was evidently one hell of a fire and Uncle Three whispered, "From the direction it's coming from, it looks like our fire all right."

I clapped my hand over his mouth as a few villagers ran towards us, yelling, "Hurry up and call the fire brigade! The mountain is about to collapse!"

I knew at once that the cave was probably collapsing from the fire and grew worried that the corpse-eaters might come crawling toward the village in droves. We whipped the mule to his full speed until his butt was swollen and finally arrived at the spot where all were gathered to fight the fire.

The villagers knew what they were doing—some of them were up ahead clearing the roads while others had begun to fetch water with their basins. They transported the water in a bucket brigade, passing it from man to man. I saw the process and figured it would take at least two hours for the basins of water to go from here to the scene of the fire. I yelled out, "Villagers, there's no need to fetch water now. This water won't put out the fire. Don't make any unnecessary sacrifices. Just wait for the fire brigade."

Everyone looked at me as though I was completely insane, and an old man responded, "Young man, this water is for the firemen to drink. If there is no drinking water at the fire, they will surely die. We'll hack down a firebreak to surround the fire. When the blaze reaches that point, there will be nothing to feed it and it will go out by itself. If you guys don't know anything, then don't burden us with your help, please." He looked at the urinals in our hands and shook his head.

Embarrassed by the stares of the villagers, I blushed

bright red. I lost face big-time, I thought, I've made a complete ass out of myself and I'll never blurt out my opinions again, Lowering my head, I followed the crowd into the forest.

After an hour's walk, we could feel the heat from the fire, and black filled the sky. The villagers took pieces of cloth, soaked them in the water, and put them over their faces. I looked at Fats, who took the silk scroll with gold trim out of his pocket, dipped it in the water, and tied it over his face. Then he picked up a shovel, joined the villagers, and began to dig a trench to serve as a firebreak.

We worked until mid-afternoon, when helicopters appeared in the sky and firefighters gathered in the forest to replace us. I was especially worried that someone would die because of our stupidity and carelessness. But fortunately, when the final count was called, only a few people had suffered minor injuries.

We returned to the village, completely exhausted. I was starving to death, asked a village child to make me two sesame seed cakes, and ate both in one bite. I had never tasted anything so savory and almost burst into tears as I swallowed them.

A village official commended us for our assistance, saying few city people were so helpful to villagers nowadays. Stop this praise, I thought, my heart cannot bear it. If you knew we were the ones to start the fire, you would certainly murder all of us.

A nurse had changed Panzi's bandages and washed his wounds. His breathing had apparently stabilized, but he had not yet regained consciousness. The doctor told me to relax, assuring me there was no danger. When the paramedics arrived later, they would take Panzi with them to a big hospital in the city, he said, and his words put me at ease.

I went back to the guesthouse with Uncle Three and took a bath. If I hadn't removed my clothes, I would never have known that not one part of my body was without injury. Every inch of my skin was either bruised or scratched. When I was fleeing for my life, I felt no pain, but the sight of my damaged flesh reminded me of what we had all been through and shot me back to reality. When I came out of the bathroom, I couldn't tell where my arms and legs stopped and the pain began.

I went to bed, fell asleep quickly, and slept until afternoon the next day. When I woke up, Fats and Uncle Three were in their beds snoring like thunder.

I went downstairs to eat breakfast and learned from my waiter that the fire had been extinguished. It was no more than a small forest fire and the troops of firefighters had already gone away.

Feeling a bit more at peace, I went to the clinic and found that Panzi had been taken to a hospital in the city of Jinan. I expressed my thanks and felt grateful but knew it was better for us not to linger in this place. It was time to leave and after a few days we returned to Jinan.

My uncle and I first went to the hospital where Panzi was hospitalized and took care of his paperwork. He was still in a coma so Uncle Three and I decided to stay with him until he was out of danger.

Fats parted with us in a hurry after we left the mountains.

29. THE PURPLE-ENAMELED GOLD BOX

He gave us a phone number where he could be reached and left the silk scroll for Uncle Three to deal with.

The next day I called the hospital and learned that Panzi still had not woken up. I sighed as Uncle Three gloomily walked into my room cursing, "God damn it, am I mad—can't believe I've been outwitted!"

I thought he meant he had been cheated in the antiques market and said, "Uncle Three, for someone with your competence and experience to be cheated must mean whatever you bought was an excellent counterfeit. There should certainly be no problem passing it on to another buyer."

Uncle Three pulled out the silk scroll with gold trimmings, barking, "Passing it on? My ass! I'm not talking about antiques. I'm talking about this thing!"

I almost fell out of bed, yelling, "What? That's not possible."

Uncle Three said, "As sure as shit it is. I sent this out to have its gold content inspected. The results show that the purity is much too high. It was simply impossible to refine gold of such high quality in that era. This is a nearly perfect counterfeit!"

I couldn't believe it. Uncle Three sighed, "I suspected it. Menyouping obviously could defeat the zombies so why did he always run away? He didn't vanquish the blood zombie until almost the last moment. He obviously wanted to get rid of us at that point and went off alone to do his own thing."

"So during the time he was separated from us, he went to the main cave and opened the coffin of the Ruler of

Dead Soldiers? And then he put this fake gold silk scroll inside? How could he do this on his own? Besides, the cave in the tree could be opened only by pulling the chains apart. If someone had opened it before us, we would have noticed their tracks," I sputtered.

"Did you look at the back of the coffin? He's a grave robber. He probably dug another cave behind the coffin, and exchanged the real gold silk script with the fake one that way!" Uncle Three sighed again. "What a pity my decades of experience couldn't see through this deception. This man is truly too deep, too unfathomable."

I still didn't understand and asked, "So the accounts I read on the scroll were all false?"

Uncle Three nodded. "These stories didn't sound credible in the first place. We were fooled by them because we were distracted by everything that had happened to us in that tomb. Now that I think back on what you read to us, I see way too many flaws. And how could you have understood only the two most important paragraphs with your level of knowledge? If you didn't understand the other ones, this clearly shows that he tampered with the ones you were able to read to make them comprehensible to you."

My mouth fell open. Uncle Three sighed again and said, "It looks like he is the only person who knows about the secret of the Ruler of the Dead Soldiers. Now that the cave has collapsed, it's impossible to go back in and find out."

Something flashed into my mind and I said, "Oh yes, I almost forgot! It wasn't completely a wasted trip. I brought something out from inside of the tomb!" Then I turned

29. THE PURPLE-ENAMELED GOLD BOX

my backpack upside down, praying that I hadn't lost it. The purple-enameled gold box was still there—I took it out and said, "It's this. I took it from the hands of the fox-corpse."

Uncle Three looked, saying, "This is a puzzle-box. The main compartment is where the locks are kept. It can't hold very much and it's quite difficult to open. You see?" he twisted the lid of the box, and its four corners opened up, showing a small turntable. There were eight holes on it, with a number in every one of them. It looked very much like an old-fashioned telephone dial.

"This is the oldest type of puzzle-box," my uncle said impatiently, "You can't open it unless you know the password. Just a minute. I'll go to that garage across the street and borrow a blowtorch—we'll cut it open and see if anything's inside."

Uncle Three ran off quickly before I could call him to come back. An eight-digit password—could it be 02200059? But how could a number printed on a foreigner's belt buckle be an ancient password? I dialed it, 0-2-2-0-0-0-5-9, heard a click, and the box opened.

END OF VOLUME ONE: CAVERN OF THE BLOOD ZOMBIES

Coming Next:
Angry Sea, Hidden Sands

VOL 2

CHAPTER ONE
THE BRONZE FISH WITH SNAKE BROWS

The lid of the box slowly opened. Inside there was space only for an object no bigger than my thumb, and what the box contained was just about that size—a small bronze fish.

I held it in my hand. The fish looked ordinary enough but the workmanship was exquisite, particularly the brows of the fish, which had been crafted to look like snakes. It was so lifelike in its appearance that I was surprised. How precious was this object and why had it been hidden for so long?

Uncle Three entered, blowtorch in hand. Startled to see the box was open, he asked, "How the hell did you do that?"

I told him about the password numbers and he frowned. "This is getting more and more confusing. It seems like that bunch of foreigners came to do more than just rob graves."

He picked up the bronze fish and his face clouded over. "What? Isn't this the Bronze Fish with Snake Brows?"

Uncle Three took something from his pocket and handed it to me. I looked at it and saw it was also a dainty little bronze fish. It too was about the size of my thumb, its brows were also shaped like snakes, and its workmanship was superb. Every last scale on its body was fine and smooth. It had to have come from the same place as the one in the purple-enameled gold box.

The only blemish in this lovely little fish was that almost embedded in between its tiny scales were bits of white grit that looked like lime. I was certain I knew where this had been found but to be sure, I asked my uncle, "Was this a marine discovery? Did you once rob an undersea tomb?"

TO BE CONTINUED IN VOLUME TWO...

Note from the Author

Back in the days when there was no television or internet and I was still a poor kid, telling stories to other children was my greatest pleasure. My friends thought my stories were a lot of fun, and I decided that someday I would become the best of storytellers.

I wrote a lot of stories trying to make that dream come true, but most of them I put away, unfinished. I completely gave up my dream of being a writer, and like many people, I sat waiting for destiny to tap me on the shoulder.

Although I gave up my dream of being a writer, luckily the dream did not give up on me. When I was 26 years old, my uncle, a merchant who sold Chinese antiques, gave me his journal that was full of short notes he had written over the years. Although fragmentary information can often be quite boring, my uncle's writing inspired me to go back to my abandoned dream. A book about a family of grave robbers began to take shape, a suspenseful novel.... I started to write again....

This is my first story, my first book that became successful beyond all expectations, a best-seller that made me rich. I have no idea how this happened, nor does anybody else; this is probably the biggest mystery of The Grave Robbers' Chronicles. Perhaps as you read the many volumes of this chronicle, you will find out why it has become so popular. I hope you enjoy the adventures you'll encounter with Uncle Three, his nephew and their companions as they roam through a world of zombies, vampires, and corpse-eaters.

Thanks to Albert Wen, Michelle Wong, Janet Brown, Kathy Mok and all my friends who helped publish the English edition of The Grave Robbers' Chronicles.

Xu Lei was born in 1982 and graduated from Renmin University of China in 2004. He has held numerous jobs, working as a graphic designer, a computer programmer, and a supplier to the U.S. gaming industry. He is now the owner of an international trading company and lives in Hangzhou, China with his wife and son. Writing isn't his day job, but it is where his heart lies.

THINGSASIAN PRESS  *Experience Asia Through the Eyes of Travelers*

"To know the road ahead, ask those coming back."
CHINESE PROVERB

Whether you're a frequent flyer or an armchair traveler, whether you are 5 or 105, whether you want fact, fiction, or photography, ThingsAsian Press has a book for you.

To Asia With Love is a series that has provided a new benchmark for travel guidebooks; for children, Asia comes alive with the vivid illustrations and bilingual text of the *Alphabetical World* picture books; cookbooks provide adventurous gourmets with food for thought. Asia's great cities are revealed through the unique viewpoints of their residents in the photographic series, *Lost and Found*. And for readers who just want a good story, ThingsAsian Press offers page-turners—both novels and travel narratives—from China, Vietnam, Thailand, India, and beyond.

With books written by people who know about Asia for people who want to know about Asia, ThingsAsian Press brings the world closer together, one book at a time.

www.thingsasianpress.com

T IS FOR TOKYO
By Irene Akio
An English-Japanese Bilingual Book

TONE DEAF IN BANGKOK
(AND OTHER PLACES)
By Janet Brown
Photographs by Nana Chen

TO NORTH INDIA WITH LOVE
A Travel Guide for the Connoisseur
Edited & with contributions by Nabanita Dutt
Photographs by Nana Chen

EXPLORING HONG KONG
A Visitor's Guide to Hong Kong Island, Kowloon,
and the New Territories
By Steven K. Bailey
Photographs by Jill C. Witt

COMMUNION
A Culinary Journey Through Vietnam
By Kim Fay
Photographs by Julie Fay Ashborn

LOST & FOUND HONG KONG
Edited by Janet McKelpin
Photographs by Hank Leung, Albert Wen, Blair Dunton,
Elizabeth Briel, and Li Sui Pong

EVERYDAY LIFE
Through Chinese Peasant Art
By Tricia Morrissey and Ding Sang Mak
An English-Chinese Bilingual Book

THE SUSHI BOOK
Everything About Sushi
By Celeste Heiter
Photographs by Marc Shultz

To Myanmar With Love
A Travel Guide for the Connoisseur
Edited & with contributions by
Morgan Edwardson
Photographs by Steve Goodman

Defiled on the Ayeyarwaddy
One Woman's Mid-life Travel Adventures on Myanmar's Great River
By Ma Thanegi

To Cambodia With Love
A Travel Guide for the Connoisseur
Edited & with contributions by Andy Brouwer
Photographs by Tewfic El-Sawy

Vignettes of Taiwan
Short Stories, Essays & Random Meditations About Taiwan
By Joshua Samuel Brown

H is for Hong Kong
A Primer in Pictures
By Tricia Morrissey;
Illustrations by Elizabeth Briel
An English-Chinese Bilingual Book

To Shanghai With Love
A Travel Guide for the Connoisseur
Edited & with contributions by Crystyl Mo
Photographs by Coca Dai

To Japan With Love
A Travel Guide for the Connoisseur
Edited & with contributions by Celeste Heiter
Photographs by Robert George

To Nepal With Love
A Travel Guide for the Connoisseur
Edited & with contributions by Cristi Hegranes
Photographs by Kraig Lieb